The Quest
of
Alinor
Dagworth

The Quest of Alinor Dagworth

Maylan Schurch

REVIEW AND HERALD® PUBLISHING ASSOCIATION
HAGERSTOWN, MD 21740

The author assumes full responsibility for the accuracy of all facts and quotations as cited in this book.

This book was
Designed by Bill Kirstein
Cover and interior illustrations by Joe Van Severen
Type set: 11.5/13 Sabon

PRINTED IN U.S.A.

98 97 96 95 94 93   10 9 8 7 6 5 4 3 2 1

R&H Cataloging Service
Schurch, Maylan Henry, 1950-
    The quest of Alinor Dagworth.

    I. Title.

        813.54

ISBN 0-8280-0738-1

CHAPTER

1

The three knights casually placed their hands on their sword hilts.

"What's he going to do to you?" Max asked me.

I was standing with my friend Max Judde in the sunlit courtyard of the king's castle. It was a bright-blue Tuesday morning, about a week after Royal Day—a perfect day to be invested as a squire.

"Will he touch your shoulder with the flat of his sword?" Max asked.

"That's only when you make somebody a knight," I said. I grinned suddenly and poked him in the ribs. "You ought to know that. You're the knighthood expert."

Max blushed. "Don't remind me."

I didn't remind him. It would have been cruel. A couple weeks ago 14-year-old Max had mapped out his whole life. First he would become a squire, then a knight, then a hardened warrior with lance and sword. Since I was only a few months younger, he'd talked me into going out to Baron Mordred's castle one morning with a bunch of other guys, at the baron's invitation, for squire training.

But then things fell apart. The baron had actually been plotting a revolution against our king. The whole thing ended OK, but Max and I almost got ourselves killed.

"Yeah," I said, shuddering. "Let's forget about last month."

"*Everything* about last month?"

"What are you talking about?"

He grinned. "You didn't know Alinor until last month."

"Max, how many times do I have to tell you that Alinor and I are just— Who's *that?*"

Max snorted. "Who's *Alinor?* Surely you know Alinor. Look over there. She's standing by my parents—"

"I don't mean *her,*" I said. "Who's that knight who just rode in over the drawbridge?"

He turned, squinted, and gave a low whistle. "From Wyndhamshire, I think. Wonder what he's doing here?"

We studied the knight carefully while he dismounted and removed his helmet. His face was grim.

Max murmured, "I don't like this."

"Here comes His Majesty," I whispered.

We turned, and Max quickly retreated to where his parents, Charles and Magda, stood smiling proudly. I grinned at them, and at Alinor beside them. She didn't smile back. Her face looked pinched and white.

The king, who happened to be Alinor's grandfather (I'll tell you about that later), had just emerged from the keep, the tower in the courtyard's center, where he lived. He was wearing a golden, gem-studded crown over his beautiful silver hair.

Following him, dressed in full chain mail and with their swords at their sides, were Sir Robert, the king's prime minister, and three other knights. It was the first time I'd seen Sir Robert in military garb.

I approached His Majesty and knelt on the stone pavement before him. His eyes crinkled in a kindly smile. "Denis, my child," he began.

He may have been a grandfather to Alinor, but he was

like a father to me. I used to be afraid and angry when I thought about him, but that was because I didn't know the truth about why he did some of the things he had to do. But now I knew, and his courage and kindness had melted my anger. A couple weeks ago he had allowed me to come and live at the castle with him. And now he stood before me in the sunlight, ready to make me his squire.

"Denis, my child," he continued, "it was I who taught you how to write. It was I who gave you the golden pen that is the mark of your order. Now it is you who must learn to teach and to give.

"Denis, my child, the way of a squire is hard. It requires you to give all of yourself in service to your people. It requires you to be ready in an instant to abandon your wishes, and even your life, so that your people might live. Do you understand this?"

"I do, Sire," I said.

"And you will understand it better as you grow," he continued. His voice strengthened until it rang throughout the vast courtyard. He now began to repeat the formula he had taught me. "Denis Anwyck, I call upon you to examine yourself."

"I have done so, Your Majesty."

"Are you willing to give yourself to your king, so that his cause may triumph?"

"I am, Your Majesty."

"Are you willing to seek within the heart of your bitterest enemy and discover treasure there?"

"I am, Your Majesty."

"Are you willing to serve without superiority, and battle without blood?"

"I am, Your Majesty."

"Then as king of this land, and knight over all knights"—he placed both his giant hands on my head—"I do, in the presence of these witnesses, name you Squire Denis Anwyck."

It was over. He held out his hand and, when I gripped it, lifted me to my feet. He embraced me. Sir Robert congratulated me, and the three other knights grinned behind their mustaches and slapped me on the back.

I glanced over my shoulder and saw the Judde family waving to me as they began to walk away across the courtyard. I motioned to them to stay around for a while, but they kept walking. Under normal chivalric codes villagers weren't invited to these events at all; besides, I knew that Max's dad, Charles, was shy in the presence of royalty.

Sir Robert, a short, stocky, balding man with a beard, shook my hand. "Congratulations, Denis. His Majesty told you that you'll be mainly in my service, didn't he?"

"Yes, Sir Robert."

"And you may be needed immediately," he whispered, rolling a thoughtful eye toward the impassive knight who watched us from beside his horse. "I don't like the looks of our visitor."

The king had noticed too. "Sir Eric," he said to one of the mustached knights, "go bid our Wyndhamshire friend welcome, and ask him his business."

But even as Sir Eric turned to obey, the visiting knight stepped quickly toward us, his spurs clicking on the flat stones. One mailed fist held a rolled-up piece of parchment bearing a red wax seal.

"Which of you is Sir Robert?" he snapped, completely ignoring His Majesty.

"I am."

"His Majesty the King of Wyndhamshire wishes me to present this to you." He thrust the parchment into Sir Robert's hands and turned away.

"Good sir," said the king.

The knight turned slowly back. "Yes?"

"May I know your name?"

"Sir John."

Sir Robert began to breathe very heavily beside me. I could tell that he was angered at the knight's abrupt discourtesy. The three mustached knights casually placed their hands on their sword hilts.

"Surely you will stay with us for a time, Sir John," said the king. "Your monarch is one of my dearest friends. I would be sadly inhospitable if I did not provide you with lodging, food, and pleasant conversation."

"This is no time for pleasant conversation," said Sir John shortly. "This is the time for war."

A pigeon fluttered down from a turret and began to pick at its shadow on the stone pavement. In the absolute stillness I could actually hear the *clack* of its beak.

"Please explain this," said the king softly.

"The parchment says it much better than I could."

Sir Robert ran his thumbnail along the red wax seal to crack it. Unrolling the parchment, he handed it, not to the king, but to me. "Read it aloud, Denis," he instructed. "It's your first official act as squire."

As my eyes fell on the words, my heart began to pound hard. The document was a declaration of war.

When I had finished reading the parchment's legal language, I handed it back to Sir Robert. He turned to Sir John.

"Your king is aware, of course, that he and Our Majesty have signed the Fortnight of Peace treaty?"

"Of course."

"And he understands that for 14 days after a declaration of war, no hostilities will take place, giving both sides an opportunity to come to a diplomatic solution?"

"Of course."

"It would aid matters, I feel," said Sir Robert heavily,

"if *all* parties"—and he leveled a stare at Sir John—"could begin by behaving with common courtesy and respect."

"Robert," murmured the king.

Sir John stared stonily at Sir Robert.

The king said, "Will you please tell the king of Wyndhamshire that no matter what has caused this desire for war, I wish for peace?"

"I will do so." The knight hesitated. Then he glanced at me. "I wish to speak without your squire present."

"Denis," said the king, "you will meet Sir Robert and me in my chambers after lunch." All trace of happiness had gone from his voice. He sounded very old. "I will probably be asking you to accompany Sir Robert to Wyndhamshire tomorrow."

"I'll be ready, Sire."

He and the prime minister and the knight turned and walked away across the courtyard.

I felt cool fingers on my arm. I turned, and found that Alinor had stayed behind the rest of the group.

During the dark times we'd experienced together last month, Alinor had been a friend and a source of strength. But now her dark blue eyes were full of fear.

"Denis," she whispered urgently, "someone is trying to kill me."

2

I stared at her. "How do you know?"

"Do you have a minute?"

"Sure. I'm free till after lunch." I glanced cautiously around. "Do you know who that knight was?"

She nodded. "Sir John of Wyndhamshire. He didn't look too cheerful."

"You bet he wasn't cheerful," I said. "Wyndhamshire is declaring war on us."

She smiled palely. "Don't joke with me, Denis. I'm scared enough as it is."

"Alli, I'm not joking. Sir John handed us a parchment, and Sir Robert had me read it out loud. In two weeks we'll be at war with them."

A small crease appeared between Alinor's delicate eyebrows. "But it can't be. Wyndhamshire's king is Grandpa's closest friend. My father and Crown Prince Andrew were like *that*." She held two fingers close together. "What's the problem?"

"I don't know," I said. "I'll probably find out after lunch. But what about you? You said someone's trying to kill you."

She grimaced. "Maybe I'm being too dramatic. Let me tell you about it."

We walked over and sat down on a bale of hay next to the huge stone courtyard wall. As I said, the king was

Alinor's grandfather. Her mother had died the way my own parents had—the Black Death—and her father, Prince Geoffrey, had been killed in Wyndhamshire about a year ago. That made Alinor the crown princess, next in line to the throne.

A month ago the king had asked some friends of his in Wyndhamshire to bring her home, but not to the castle. She was staying with the baron's wife in a house in the village so that she could have a chance to mingle with the townspeople. Nobody (except me and a few people at the castle) knew who she really was, not even the baroness.

Now, as I stared at her, I remembered how last month when I was going through my crisis, she was calm and cool. But now she was the one who was afraid.

"Just before I came up to the castle this morning," she began, "a street vendor knocked at the door, selling pastries. He asked me if my name was Alinor, and I said yes. He gave me one of his sugared cakes as a sample, and I thanked him. He said goodbye and left. As I was turning to go inside the house, I dropped the cake on the threshold. And Marie got it."

"Who's Marie?"

"The baroness's lapdog. She snatched it and gobbled it up."

I chuckled. "Too bad."

She looked at me gravely. "Yes. As soon as she'd eaten the cake, she fell over in convulsions."

I blinked. "Convulsions?"

"She lay there twitching and gagging, her eyes rolled back in her head." Alinor put her hand on my arm. "Do you know what I think, Denis?"

"What?"

"I think that cake was poisoned."

14

I tugged doubtfully at my earlobe. "You can't be sure of that."

"If you'd seen the way Marie carried on—"

"Well, how's she doing now? Did she die?"

Alinor gulped. "I don't know. The baroness was in the room behind me, and she hurried over and knelt down and started crying over the dog. Then I guess I just panicked. I left them both there, and ran up here to the castle."

"So you don't know how Marie's doing?"

"No."

"Maybe a piece of the cake got caught in her throat."

"But her eyes were rolling back in her head."

"I've seen dogs' eyes do that when they're choking on a bone."

"Well," said Alinor doubtfully, "maybe so. But it was weird." She stood up.

"Want me to walk you back to the village?"

She shook her head. "Better not. I'm leaving the castle by the secret entrance anyway, so nobody will get suspicious." (We'd often used this secret doorway when we wanted to talk to the king.)

I stood up too. "How long is His Majesty going to keep it quiet that you're a princess?"

"I'm not sure," she said. "He just keeps telling me that he wants me to learn to live among the people of the village, and that one of these days he wants to tear down his castle and do the same." She scuffed the stone pavement with her shoe. "He was hoping he'd never need a castle again. But now all this has to happen."

"The war?"

"Yes," she groaned. "And it's really so silly, anyway. Nobody can do anything to us. Our country is protected on three sides by mountains, and on the fourth by a river. Wyndhamshire can't get *to* us, at least not with an army."

"But they're dead serious about it," I said. "Oh, by the

way, it looks like I'll be going to Wyndhamshire tomorrow."

She turned her head quickly to look at me. "Why?"

"To act as scribe for Sir Robert."

"Denis, you'll be safe, won't you?"

"Oh, I'll be safe," I assured her. "I just wish I knew what the problem is."

"So do I."

After lunch I found out.

"Denis," the king said to me when Sir Robert and I were seated at a table with him in his chambers, "you might as well know everything. Has Alinor told you much about her parents?"

"Not much, Sire. I understand her mother died of the Black Death. She also told me that her father was killed a year ago in a jousting tournament."

The king frowned thoughtfully. "That's what I thought until this morning. If Sir John can be trusted—and I believe he can—my Geoffrey was killed in some kind of private duel."

Sir Robert shook his head. "That part just doesn't ring true, Your Majesty. Your son was an expert swordsman, but he would never duel to defend his honor."

"That's what I keep saying to myself," said the king. "But whether he did or not, my good friend the Wyndhamshire king believes it. And what's worse, he believes that Geoffrey didn't fight fair, but committed cold-blooded murder." His Majesty stood to his feet and began to pace the room. "Robert, this is a tragedy. It has come between me and my friend."

"I know, Your Majesty."

"I had such high hopes when I sent Geoffrey to Wyndhamshire. I wanted him to spread my ideas of freedom and choice and equality. This century has seen too many wars. Too many castles stand on too many hills."

"But we made progress," said Sir Robert.

"We did," admitted the king. "Geoffrey was so successful that my friend the Wyndhamshire king actually forsook his own castle and began to live in a palace in the town. It was a great triumph for human history. And one of these days, when Baron Mordred's threat is over, I'm going to do the same thing."

"Sire," I asked, "do you think the baron has anything to do with this?"

The king shrugged. "Probably. But if Mordred wants to take over the kingdom, why would he want to stir up hostilities with Wyndhamshire at the same time?"

"They might help him overthrow you," suggested Sir Robert.

The king shook his head in a dissatisfied way. "I will not give up hope," he said.

He turned to me. "Denis, I am asking you to accompany Sir Robert to Wyndhamshire. You will act as his scribe. You will record in your book each day's events, including details of the negotiations. If all else fails, we will at least have an accurate record of our efforts."

"It's a pity you yourself cannot also go, Your Majesty," said Sir Robert.

The king nodded. "I want to go. But to leave the country while Mordred is still at large would be fatal. Literally. Fatal to the peace of the land, and probably fatal to my life." His lips tightened. "Mordred is a menace, as we have found out this past month. He must not be allowed to continue forever."

He stood up. "Robert," he said, "send a messenger to the Bocks. You remember Bock, don't you? He was Geoffrey's squire, and a very devoted one. He and his wife are retired in the town of Ashton, about two miles from Wyndhamshire. I'd like to arrange that you stay in their farmhouse. I think their home will be safer than the city."

CHAPTER

A s Sir Robert and I talked with the king in his chambers, dramatic things were happening to Alinor in the baroness's town house. She told me about it later.

When she arrived home from the castle and let herself in through the front door of the three-story mansion, a maid with a broom said, "The baroness wants to see you, Miss Alinor."

"Thanks, Clara. Where is she?"

"In the sewing room, miss."

Alinor slowly climbed the stairs to a sunlit room on the third floor. The baroness was seated by the window, working on some embroidery.

"How's Marie doing?" Alinor asked as she entered.

"Oh, there you are, dear," chirped the baroness. She was a pink-cheeked, rather fluffy-minded little woman. "Much better, thank goodness. She's actually chewing on some table scraps in the kitchen, poor sweet darling. I simply do not know what came over her."

Alinor looked at the floor. "I'm sorry I ran away so fast."

"Oh, that's fine, dear. Naturally you were frightened."

Alinor glanced up quickly. "Frightened?"

"About Marie." The baroness blinked at her. "Weren't you?"

"Oh, I—guess so." Alinor walked over to the sewing table and picked up her own embroidery work, a sampler on which she had carefully printed the motto "If You Would Wear a Royal Crown, Forsake Your Castle, Tear It Down." She sat down, threaded a new needle, and started work on the upper left arm of the first Y.

The baroness began to talk again. She liked to talk. Her chatter often bored Alinor, who instead of listening would often wander away down obscure alleyways in her own mind.

Fortunately, the baroness never required much response from her audience. During the past month Alinor had become expert in murmuring an encouraging "Oh?" or "Uh-huh?" or even a "Wow!" according to the voice tones of the older woman. Each response would set the baroness prattling happily on for another 15 minutes or so. It was really rather restful.

"Yes, Marie is so much better now," twittered the baroness. "I cannot think what could have happened to the poor baby. She's always been such a healthy little thing, always so perky and bright. She always jumps up on my bed first thing in the morning—frankly, my dear, far earlier than I myself would like to get up, especially when it's cold outside . . ."

Alinor's thoughts drifted elsewhere.

A cold, worried lump began to form itself in the pit of her stomach as she thought about war with Wyndham-shire. What reason would they have to become hostile like this? And with this country's natural protection, what good would it do them?

". . . and it was such a surprise to me to see her like that, her little tongue hanging out of her mouth, and gasping."

"Wow!" said Alinor gravely.

She began to be very homesick for Wyndhamshire, and

for her father and mother, who lay side by side in the gray cemetery next to the royal palace. She wished she could take Denis back there and show him where she grew up . . .

". . . and so I said to her, 'Jane, I can't thank you enough for what you have done.' "

Jane? With a jerk Alinor came back to the present. She looked curiously at the baroness. Evidently the conversation had shifted to a new topic, someone named Jane.

"Interesting," murmured Alinor.

"What, dear?"

"I said it was interesting."

"Oh—yes, certainly. What a talent she had."

"Jane, you mean?"

"Yes."

"A talent for what?" Alinor asked.

The baroness's eyebrows rose in mild astonishment. "Oh, didn't I make myself clear? I was just telling you, my dear. A talent for healing."

"Oh," said Alinor, hoping for more.

"Yes," continued the baroness, "how lucky it was that she just happened to be passing by when Marie became so ill. After Jane had worked with her awhile, Marie raised her little head and looked around the room—I think she was looking for her mummy, and so I said, 'Right here, Meemee, right here. Mummy's close by.' And then she settled right back to sleep. It reminded me of the time when she was just a little puppy, so darling, precious, and tiny, and one day I was sitting with her out there on that garden seat, you know? The stone bench just over beyond the roses?"

"Wow!" said Alinor, who was already beginning to drift back into her thoughts. If only Sir Eric could go along with Denis and Sir Robert. Sir Robert was getting older, and she wasn't sure how good he'd be with self-defense. If only Denis knew a little more about sword fighting. But he was like her father. Father had been an expert swordsman, but he had hated to fight.

". . . so I said, 'Jane, I'm sure Miss Alinor would love to have you.' "

Alinor's needle stabbed her finger severely. "What?" she asked breathlessly. "What's that? I'm sorry—I didn't catch that."

The baroness smiled sweetly. "I asked Jane if she would like to join our staff as your personal maid. I said, 'I'm sure Miss Alinor would love—' "

"But," Alinor interrupted, "you didn't—I mean, I don't really need—what I'm trying to say is No, please. Thank you very much, but I'd rather not."

The baroness looked puzzled. "No, dear?"

"You see, I—I'm just not used to the idea of having a servant."

"But dear, it's time you learned how to handle the domestic staff. And," said the baroness, as if this were the crowning delight, "Jane is almost exactly your age. You two would have such fun together."

"But—"

"Always, of course," admonished the older lady, "making sure that you don't let her step over the line. Jane is really little more than an orphan street child. You must never allow her to become too close to you. You must say to her quite plainly, 'Jane, let us remember just who I am and who you are.' I remember when I was your age, I had to do the same with little Maggie. 'Maggie,' I said—and my heart was in my mouth, I was so scared—'Maggie—' "

Alinor broke in. "I'd really rather not, if you don't mind," she said as sweetly as she could.

"But why not, my dear?"

"Because—" Alinor wanted so much to burst out into one of her grandfather's passionate speeches about equal freedom and dignity for everyone. The words arranged themselves on the tip of her tongue.

"My dear"—behind the soft twittery voice there was a touch of steel, probably the same steel that had success-fully put little Maggie in her place—"when my friends in Wyndhamshire asked me to allow you to come here, I received the distinct impression that they wished me to fit you for your duties as one of the nobility."

"Yes," said Alinor, "but—"

"And I will be the first to admit that Jane has many rough edges. She is quite plain-spoken and will need to be solidly trained. I will help you there. But she does have a good heart. I'm sure you'll learn to love her."

Alinor's voice rose almost to a wail. "I can take care of myself, really."

"My dear—"

"I don't need a maid."

"Oh, dear," sighed the baroness. Then she brightened. "Why not call her a companion, then?"

Alinor was silent. She jerked the thread until the embroidered Y crumpled.

"Won't you at least consent to meet her, my dear?"

"Oh, all right," sighed Alinor.

4

Alinor told me later that the first thing she noticed about Jane, when the baroness ushered the girl into the sewing room, was that she was remarkably thin. The second was that Jane's dress was too small.

"Jane," chirped the baroness, "this is Miss Alinor. You must remember to call her Miss Alinor when you speak to her."

"Hi," said Jane.

"Jane?" cooed the baroness warningly.

"Hi, *Miss Alinor*," said Jane quickly. She stared unblinkingly at Alinor with solemn brown eyes that were hard and streetwise. Her short brown hair hung in curled tangles.

"I think," murmured the baroness, "that, 'Good day, Miss Alinor' would perhaps be just a mite nicer. Why don't you practice it, Jane?"

"Good day, Miss Alinor."

"Good day, Jane," said Alinor.

"Why doesn't she call me 'Miss Jane'?" Jane asked scornfully.

"Let me explain, dear," said the older lady. And while she did so, Alinor bit her lip very hard to keep from joining in the conversation.

"So now do you understand?" asked the baroness at length.

"I guess so, Miss Baroness," said Jane.

Alinor had to bend her head down to keep from laughing.

The baroness sighed. "Well, Jane, for just a minute or two I'm going to leave you here with Miss Alinor. I'm sure that you two will get along very well together." She hurried out of the room.

Alinor looked at Jane. Jane looked at Alinor.

Alinor cleared her throat. "How old are you, Jane?"

"Twelve and a half. How old are you?" asked Jane. "Miss Alinor," she added hastily.

"Thirteen."

"I hate this dress," Jane said, looking down at herself. "It's too small. It's not too modest either. But it's cool."

Alinor eyed Jane's thin frame a bit enviously. Then she said, "Have you asked your parents if you can be my maid?"

Jane's eyes fell. "They're dead."

"So are mine."

"*Are* they?" Jane looked up with interest and sympathy in her brown eyes. "The Black Death?"

Alinor winced and nodded. "My mother died of it. My dad died in a tournament."

"My dad and mom *both* died from the Black Death. Do you have a boyfriend?"

Alinor's face reddened at the sudden change in topic. She opened her mouth, but before she could decide on a diplomatic way to say "It's none of your business," the baroness hurried in again, carrying two or three dresses.

"Jane," she said, "come with me. I have some clothes that my daughter wore when she was still at home. She was about your size. Let's go find out if they fit."

They left, and Alinor got up and wandered over to the window. *What a way to ruin a day*, she was thinking. The last thing on earth she wanted was to be saddled with a

maid. Even Grandpa, the king of the country, did everything for himself. The people at the castle were salaried
working persons, not slaves. What would Grandpa do if he
were in her position?

Probably, she thought wryly, *he'd have already made
friends with her*. "Alinor," he had often told her, "we are
in this world not to make things comfortable for ourselves,
but to make life happier for others."

For several minutes she stood in thought, her eyes
seeing nothing beyond the windowframe. Then they suddenly focused, and she saw the pastry vendor again. He
had come from behind the building across the street, and
as her gaze met his, he melted out of sight again.

Alinor stepped away from the window, breathing
quickly. All the fear she'd felt earlier came rushing back.
Who was he? Why was he there? Was he watching for her?

"Does it fit you, Jane?" came the baroness's voice. She
entered the room, and a startlingly transformed Jane
followed her. Something very nice had happened to her
brown curls, and she was wearing a dress that, while it
didn't quite hide her tomboyish swagger, was definitely an
improvement.

"Yeah," said Jane happily.

"Jane, you must really call me, 'my lady.' "

"OK, your lady."

"*My* lady," corrected the baroness wearily. "Jane, you
must remember that you are in the baron's home, and
there will be all sorts of exalted visitors who will stay here
from time to time. You will want them to think well of
you."

"Gotcha, my lady."

I must not laugh, thought Alinor firmly.

"Now, girls," sighed the baroness, "I must leave you
alone again. I must supervise preparations for dinner."

There was a silence when she'd gone. It was an

awkward one for Alinor, but for Jane it was the perfect opportunity to stare steadily at her new mistress, examining her from her dark-gold curls to her sturdy walking shoes.

"I wish *I* was a blonde," she said wistfully.

"Oh?"

"I mean, I wish I was a blonde, *Miss Alinor*. Yeah," sighed Jane. "My boyfriend might take more of an interest in me if I was a blonde. Do you have a boyfriend?"

"Jane, that's really none of your business."

"Who is he?"

"I said," murmured Alinor dangerously, "that it's none of your business. And call me 'Miss Alinor.' "

"Well, sorry I *asked*," sniffed Jane, offended. "Miss Alinor."

There was another silence. Alinor was a bit ashamed of herself for being so defensive. After all, this girl was one of the village people her grandfather had sent her here to learn to live among. *I've kept myself pretty sheltered here in the baroness's town house,* she thought.

"The baroness tells me you cured Marie," she said in a pleasant voice.

"Sure," said Jane cheerfully. "Nothing to it."

"How did you do it?"

"I made her eat some of the leaves off that bush out behind the garden."

"*Leaves?*"

"Yeah."

"But how did you make her eat them?"

Jane giggled. "I just wadded them up and stuffed them down her throat. She didn't have much choice. Miss Alinor," she added quickly.

"How did you know those leaves would work?"

Jane gazed at her in surprise, as if she were startled that there could be someone so out-of-touch as not to know how to cure dogs in their death agonies. "Oh, I just knew it."

"But who taught you?"

"Nobody taught me," said Jane. "I just keep my eyes open and notice what works."

Alinor paused. She'd suddenly had an idea. "Jane," she said, "what do you think was wrong with Marie?"

"Somebody poisoned her." Jane said flatly.

Alinor gulped. "Are you sure?"

"Sure, I'm sure," Jane said. "Miss Alinor, I mean. I'm sorry I don't keep calling you Miss Alinor. It sounds so — so —"

"Don't worry about it," said Alinor quickly. "Just remember to do it when the baroness is around. But how can you be so sure the dog was poisoned? Maybe she was just choking on — on whatever she was eating."

"I knew by looking at the yuck that came up after she ate the leaves," said Jane frankly. "And another thing," she said, "this house is being watched."

The back of Alinor's neck prickled, but she responded casually. "It is?"

"Yeah. Yesterday and today," Jane said. "It's this tall guy with a false beard. Sometimes he pretends he's a cookie vendor, but most of the time he just stands over there back of that building across the street."

She went over and peered out the window. "There he is now. No," she said thoughtfully, "he just stepped behind that building again." She turned away from the window. "He probably saw me looking out. He keeps watching the house carefully, but if he sees somebody come out, he's gone like a flash."

For a moment more Alinor stood staring across the street. Suddenly she turned. "Jane," she said.

"What?"

"You may be my maid if you want to. But I'm not

going to call you a maid. I'm going to call you a 'companion.' "

"What's that?"

"And Jane," said Alinor, her eyes sparkling, "tomorrow, you and I are going to travel to Wyndhamshire. And above all," she said earnestly, "whatever you do, do not say anything about this to the baroness."

At almost the exact moment Alinor announced to Jane that they were going to Wyndhamshire, I was in the castle stables cinching my stallion's saddle. Mounting him, I clattered out over the old drawbridge, the backpack with my writing materials jouncing behind me.

As I glanced up at the rusty drawbridge support chains, I felt depressed. They were rusty because nobody had tipped the bridge up to a closed position since the old, dark days before the present king's rule. But if things got worse with Wyndhamshire, the servants would have to come out and oil those chains and repair the two giant winches that wound them.

And maybe someone would even have to reinstall the old portcullis, the toothed iron gate that had once hung poised above the main archway, ready to crash down on the heads of approaching enemies.

As I trotted down into the village and along Max's street, the familiar surroundings helped me lose some of my gloom. Arriving at the Juddes' house, I jumped off the horse and tied it to a tree.

The front door was open. "Magda, are you home?" I called.

Up until a week ago I'd lived here. Back when I was 5 my parents died from the Black Death, and the king had sent his soldiers to take me away. They'd brought me here, to the home of Charles Judde, woodworker.

His wife, Magda, had scooped me up in her arms and made me her son, even though they already had a boy nearly a year older than me.

"Denis!" boomed a familiar voice, and there stood Magda in the doorway. She threw her arms around me, and for a second or two it was like old times again.

Then she held me out at arm's length. "How are you, anyway?"

"Fine," I said. "And you?"

She snorted. "Listen to him," she said. "A week in the castle and he's talking just like a noble. 'And you?' " she mimicked. Then she grabbed my ribs and tickled me. "That'll take the starch out of you."

I roared with helpless laughter. Escaping from her, I dashed out to the backyard. There, just as I'd been hoping, were Max and his dad, working on a brand-new long wagon.

"Dad!" shouted Max. "Here's Denis!"

"Aha," said Charles with difficulty, because he had several nails in his mouth. Removing them, he smiled his slow smile. "Hey, there, squire. What brings you down here? Haven't seen you for about a week now."

"You saw me this morning," I said.

"Yeah," said Charles, "but not to talk to. Hey. That reminds me. Who was that knight who showed up just as things were coming to a close?"

His Majesty and I had talked about how much to tell the Juddes, so I knew what I could say.

"That's why I'm here," I said. "That was a Wyndhamshire knight. Sir Robert and I have to make a trip over there. We've got to start soon, like tonight, and we might be gone a couple weeks."

"The country of Wyndhamshire or the city?" asked

Charles. Wyndhamshire is the name of both the country and its capital city.

"To Wyndhamshire the city."

Max stared at me enviously. "You'll be there for two weeks?"

"And," I said, "the king heard about your new long wagon and wanted to know if he could rent it. He wants something like this so we won't have to depend on local inns. This way we can travel by our own schedule."

Charles raised his eyebrows. "So they've heard about my wagon up at the castle?" He sounded pleased. "Actually, I am rather proud of it. Come and look."

We walked around the wagon. It was shaped like a large box, about 10 feet long, six wide, and six high. The upper half of the walls were pieces of hard-cured leather sewn together, and the roof was waterproof canvas. Up at the front was a high bench for the driver.

"Pretty fancy, eh?" Charles said. "It's light but strong. That means it can carry several passengers with only two horses."

Max opened a leather door in the side and climbed inside. "Come on in, Denis."

"This is fantastic," I said. "These little candle brackets on the walls. And the two bunk hammocks."

"And here's a bench two or three people can sit on," said Max. "I built that. And these canvas bags hanging on the walls are for baggage."

"This would be perfect," I said to Charles, who was standing just outside the door. "Would you mind if we used it?"

"Not at all," said Charles. "It'll be the perfect road test. I'm planning to build several of these and sell them."

"And Dad's going to pay me a salary," said Max. "I'm going to get a commission on every one he sells."

"Calm down, Max," Charles said. "Don't count your

carriages before they're built."

"But you promised, Dad."

"Sure, I promised. But don't be so money-hungry."

"I'm not money-hungry," protested Max.

"Money will come, but only after a lot of hard work and quality workmanship."

Max said nothing.

"Speaking of money," I said, "the king wants to know what your rental price is."

Charles thought a moment. "He can use it for free."

"No." I shook my head firmly. "The king wants to pay fair rental value, and more."

"Oh, I'm not letting it go for free," he said. "There's a condition."

"What's that?"

"That you allow Max to come along."

Max gasped. "Dad! Can I?"

"Yes. Quite a while now I've been thinking about sending you to Wyndhamshire, but I didn't know how to get you there and back safely."

"Wow!" Max shouted. "This is terrific!"

"Hey, *hey*!" Charles spoke seriously. "It's not going to be a vacation, Max."

"No?"

"No. What I want you to do once you get there is to borrow some drawing paper from Denis and visit the woodworking shops. I want you to make sketches of new furniture styles. I want you to learn better ways of fastening wood together. Then I want you to bring all that back here and teach *me*."

Max nodded slowly. "Sure. I could do that," he said. Then he turned to me. "When do we start?"

"Tonight."

Charles frowned. "I heard you say that, but I thought you were joking."

"No, that's true."

"Why?"

"That's the way the king wants it."

Charles stared at me. "You'll never make it over the mountains in the dark."

"Oh, we're not going that far tonight," I said. "We just want to get on the road as soon as possible."

"Denis, is something going on?"

I said nothing.

"Glad I'm not involved in all that stuff," Charles said finally. "By the way, I'll send along enough extra wood so Max can make repairs if something breaks."

"So you really could have it ready this evening?" I asked. "Like maybe 10:00?"

"It's ready now," Charles said. "Max, you'd better go inside and start deciding what you want to take with you."

On the way back to the castle I stopped at the baroness's town house. A slender brown-haired girl I didn't know opened the door. She stared at me without blinking.

"Hi," she said. "I mean, good day, sir."

"Is Miss Alinor in?" I asked.

To my surprise, she grinned a bit mockingly and looked at me with interest.

"Yeah," she said. "Who do I say wants to see her?"

"Denis," I said. *Strange maid*, I thought to myself.

Alinor came quickly down. Stepping outside, she firmly closed the door.

"Who's that new girl?" I asked.

Alli rolled her eyes. "Jane. My new companion."

"I thought you were all for freedom and equality."

"Don't rub it in," she said. "The baroness made me take her on." She giggled. "I hope she treated you properly. The baroness has been coaching her on the titles of everyone from squires to royalty."

"She needs a little polish," I admitted. "But to change

the subject, it looks like we're heading out tonight. Max is going too. His dad wants him to check out the Wyndham-shire woodworking shops."

"H'mmm," said Alinor.

"So I just came to say goodbye."

"Oh, don't say goodbye."

I blinked. "Why not?"

"We're coming along. Jane and I."

y jaw went slack. "What?"

"Jane and I are coming to Wyndhamshire with you."

"But you can't."

"Yes, we can."

I lowered my voice and glanced around. "His Majesty won't even consider it for a minute."

"Why not?"

"Alinor, this trip is going to be fast and dangerous."

"No more dangerous than staying right here. I almost got poisoned this morning."

"We went over all that. The dog was probably just choking."

"Not according to Jane."

"Your new maid?"

"My new companion."

"What does she know?"

In a few quick words she told me how Jane had cured Marie.

"Well, hey," I said, relieved, "now that you've got a companion to help look out for you there's no need for you to come to Wyndhamshire."

Alinor's lips tightened. "We're coming with you."

I threw out my hands in exasperation. "If you don't

feel safe, why not go up to the castle and stay with His Majesty?"

"Denis, use your head," whispered Alinor tensely. "That would blow my cover for sure. The baroness would catch on right away. Even if she didn't, she'd tell the baron and he'd get suspicious. No," she said firmly, "we're coming along."

"But—"

"Another reason I want to go," she said softly, "is to visit the graves of my parents. Because if war breaks out in two weeks, who knows if I'll ever get back there again?"

I paused. "Come up to the castle then, and ask the king."

"You ask him—but promise me you'll give him all my reasons. Please let him know how badly I want to go. Do you promise?"

I shrugged helplessly. "I promise."

She smiled at me. It was the first time I'd seen her smile today. She put her hand on my arm. "Thank you, Denis."

To my vast surprise, the king agreed with her. "If she's really being watched," he mused, "it may be the baron's plot. In that case, it's not wise to have her in the baron's town house. And if we can launch your group tonight without the baron or his wife knowing anything about it, she may be actually better off than if she stayed."

Now that I looked at it that way, the idea made sense. "I'll go and tell her now, Sire."

"Wait a moment. I want you to promise me one thing."

"Yes, Sire?"

"I am going to put her in your care. I want you to watch over her carefully."

"I'll do my best, Sire."

"I know you're still a boy. And, of course, I'll tell Robert to keep an eye on her too. But please, make it your personal responsibility to not let her come to any harm."

"I'll try not to, Sire."

"Her parents' graves are near the palace, and that may be dangerous ground. Please make sure that you are with her when she goes there. Will you promise me that?"

"I promise."

He turned to look out the window at the green countryside beyond the walls. "All may yet be well. I do not know what is behind Wyndhamshire's warmongering. I don't know what part, if any, Mordred plays in this. But I do know this," and he turned to face me again, "I do not wish to lose my granddaughter to my enemy."

So I made my way back to the town house, and after again facing a very interested Jane, who subjected me to an even more careful scrutiny than before, I told Alinor the news she wanted to hear.

She told me later that Jane was excited too.

"Jane, we can go," she said after she'd closed the door behind me.

"Great!" squeaked Jane, and threw her arms around Alinor and kissed her. Then she blushed and jumped back. "I'm sorry, Miss Alinor, I didn't mean—"

Alinor, a bit shaken at the sudden attack, cleared her throat and adjusted her hair. "That's all right. I'm glad you're going along."

"Oh, I've always wanted to see Wyndhamshire. I never ever thought I'd get there."

"It's a nice place," Alinor said wistfully. "I grew up there. And I want to go see my parents' graves."

"I'll help you find them," Jane promised.

"Thanks, but I know where they are."

"You do? I can't always find my folks' graves. I always have to feel around in the weeds for a couple stones I laid on top of them."

Alinor suddenly burst into tears.

Concerned, Jane came close to her. "Alinor—Miss

Alinor, I mean—did I say something wrong?"

"No," Alinor sobbed.

"I don't know much about being a companion. You'll have to teach me some more."

"No, you're doing fine."

"Why are you crying?"

"I don't know."

"Do you miss your mom and dad?"

"Oh, yes . . . yes, very much."

"I miss mine too." And Jane began to cry.

"Oh, dear," said Alinor 10 minutes later. "We'd better wash our faces. The baroness might come along. Remember now, not a hint to her that we're leaving tonight."

"OK. I'll help you pack."

As night drew on, Alinor and Jane spelled each other at their lookout post in the sewing room window, watching to see if the loiterer was there. Their packing was made more difficult because the baroness wasn't an early-to-bed kind of person. They tiptoed around as quietly as they could, but twice they heard a birdlike voice calling, "Girls? Girls? Shouldn't you be getting to bed pretty soon?"

Alinor scrutinized the dresses the baroness had given Jane. "You can wear these until we get to Wyndhamshire," she told her companion, "and then I'll buy you some new ones."

They tied everything in bundles. At the last minute, Jane added a small cloth bag that had a spicy odor. "Leaves and other stuff," she told Alinor, "just in case."

The two girls crept cautiously out the servants' entrance at the back of the town house. A bright moon shone down, so they took the back alleys, hurrying along in the inky shadows. Finally they entered the driveway that led into Max's backyard, where he and I stood with Sir Robert, Charles, and Magda.

"Alinor! Over here," I hissed.

We rapidly introduced Jane to the rest of the group and prepared to depart. The wagon stood ready. Max and I had harnessed two of the king's horses to it. Angel, Alinor's own horse, was tied to the rear of the wagon, along with my stallion.

Charles solemnly shook our hands and told us to be careful. Magda, who had raided her store of nuts and dried fruit, placed a large bag of these in one of the canvas baggage-sacks on the wall. She kissed the girls and Max and me (despite our reluctance) and shooed us up into the carriage.

Max had lit the wall candles and their warm glow made the carriage incredibly cozy. The girls sat side by side on the lower hammock bunk, and Max and I took the bench. The carriage shifted, and I knew that Sir Robert had ascended to the driver's seat.

"OK," came the hushed tones of Charles from outside, "I think she's travelworthy and ready to go. Good luck!"

"Thank you very much, Mr. Judde," said Sir Robert in a barely audible voice. "His Majesty is very grateful to you and will not forget your kindness."

Then we were off. We rumbled through the streets, and then I could tell by the gritty sound under the wheels that we'd come to the main road. After we'd traveled for a few minutes, the wall candles flickering, we suddenly heard the voice of Sir Robert outside. He spoke quietly, but there was alarm in his tone.

"What does this mean? Who are you?"

The carriage came to a jolting stop.

7

Inside the candlelit carriage, the four of us stared at each other, terrified.

"Who is it?" Alinor whispered.

"Shhh." Max cocked his head. "Listen."

The carriage shifted. Sir Robert had dismounted. We heard a few muffled words, then more silence. Then a rattle at the door, and a tug, and it opened.

I happened to be watching Alinor as the door swung out. I saw her expression change from fear to gasping relief as a figure in a striped, hooded robe entered and crouched before us. His face was in shadow.

"Your Majesty," I gulped.

Jane hiccuped and shrank back against the carriage wall.

"Yes," the king said, throwing back his hood. The candles gleamed on his silver hair and beard. He smiled. "I must not be here long; I may have been followed. But I wanted to say good-bye."

"I wish you could come too," whispered Alinor.

Jane looked at her curiously.

His Majesty glanced thoughtfully at Jane, then said to his granddaughter, "Thank you, young lady. I wish I could too. But please remember one thing: even though I am not with you, I have many things under my control. If you

follow the directions I have given Sir Robert, you will be safe."

He turned to Max. "Max, you are an expert workman."

"Thank you, Sire."

"Remember that lives depend on the travelworthiness of your father's carriage." He looked at me. "Denis?"

"Yes, Sire."

"Remember what I have told you."

"I will, Sire."

"Alinor," he said gently.

"Yes— Your Majesty."

"You have suffered much, and you will suffer more. But suffer wisely, not foolishly."

She paused, eyeing him gravely, almost challengingly. Then her eyes fell and she said, "Yes, Your Majesty."

"And Jane," murmured the king.

Jane's eyes grew bigger. In a tiny whisper she said, "You know my name?"

He smiled at her. "I understand you are a healer."

Jane just stared at him, her lips trembling.

"Jane, your eyes are sharp and your mind is quick. While you are in Wyndhamshire your eyes must be doubly sharp and your mind triply quick. Take good care of your mistress."

Jane's eyebrows came together for just a second in a curious frown. She glanced from the king to Alinor and back again. "Sure, Your Majesty."

"Thank you." He reached for the door handle, opened it again, and was gone.

Alinor half-rose as if to follow him, but then settled back onto the hammock and broke into sobs. Jane, still looking dazed, awkwardly put her arm around her. And the carriage rumbled onward into the night.

Around midnight Sir Robert guided the carriage into a

dense grove of trees. We slept for a few hours in a clearing under the stars, some distance from the wagon.

Sir Robert woke us when the east was barely alight. "Let's go," he said. "We can eat as we ride, thanks to Mrs. Judde's dried fruit."

We untied Angel and my stallion from the back of the wagon, and the girls and Max and I took turns riding them. The less weight in the wagon as we ascended the northern mountains the easier it would be for the two horses who had to pull it.

It was a tremendously difficult climb, and I could see how well-protected our country was from military attack. By nightfall we still hadn't reached the top, so again we slept until the first light of dawn.

Finally, late in the afternoon of the third day, we were through the mountain passes and crossing the level golden wheatfields of the country of Wyndhamshire. (The country and its capital city bore the same name.) The royal blue sky cradled a sun burning brightly in the west.

It was while we were traveling along a narrow road that the accident happened. I was sitting beside Sir Robert on the driver's bench, holding the reins. Max was inside, and the girls had ridden on ahead. Suddenly there was a sharp crack, and the carriage box sagged to the left, almost pitching me off my seat. Sir Robert grabbed the reins from me.

"Stop the horses!" Max cried from inside. "Set the brake!"

The carriage grated to a halt and Max emerged. He swung himself underneath and groaned. "Oh, great! Just like I thought. The left underbrace."

"Broken?" I asked.

"Yeah," he said bitterly. "What did you hit, anyway?"

"I didn't see anything," said Sir Robert.

Max whooshed his breath out in a sigh. "I've got a

spare brace along, but I can't do anything permanent until I have a lot more time. This wasn't supposed to happen. You must have hit something really big."

I craned my neck to peer at the road behind. "No way. All I can see is a little rock about the size of my fist."

Max squinted at it. "Yeah, I can see the wheel track in the dust. You went right over it. But that shouldn't have broken the brace."

"Can you do anything at all?" asked Sir Robert.

"Sure, I can jerry-rig it," Max said, "but we can't go fast. You'll both have to help me lift it on this side. I'll get the prop blocks."

After the horses were unhitched and the carriage propped up, Max said, "Denis and I can take it from here, Sir Robert."

"Fine," said the knight. He mounted one of the horses and rode ahead to tell the girls what had happened.

As Max worked, he told me about his dreams. "What a lucky break to be able to go to Wyndhamshire."

"I hope you get a lot of good furniture ideas."

He grunted. "I don't want furniture ideas, I want cash."

"Dream on, buddy. They don't hand out free cash in Wyndhamshire."

"Maybe not," he said, "but there's probably lots of easier ways to make money than carving table legs all day."

"Like what?"

"Like—well, anything," he said. "Push up on that brace. Like that. OK. One more nail here, and then some leather lashing, and that should hold it for a while." He worked expertly for a few minutes more, then rolled out from under the carriage and sat up. "But one thing's for sure. I'm not going to be a hammer jockey all my life."

"But that's what you're trained in. You've got the skills."

"Would you like to be a woodworker?"

I thought for a second. "Probably not."

"Then don't try to force me into it. It's easy for you to talk, sitting there on your duff with your pen squiggling over the paper."

"Max," I objected, "I'm not trying to force you into anything. It's just that you've got the skills for woodworking, and I've got the skills for writing."

"Lucky," he muttered.

"Hey—say the word, and I'll teach you. Probably take you six, seven months at most. Then you can be a scribe too."

He shook his head in a dissatisfied way. "No, I want my cash quicker than that. There's got to be a way to make some easy money." He waved to Sir Robert and the two girls, who were approaching us. "Carriage is fixed!" he called out. "We can start!"

That night a low, black layer of clouds arose from the northwest.

"We're in for a prairie thunderstorm," said Sir Robert. "Girls, you'll be safe inside. Max, do you have any extra hammocks?"

"Sure. In one of the luggage bags."

"Good. String three of them under the wagon, between the axles. No sleeping on the ground tonight."

Soon the storm was upon us. Lightning flashed, thunder crackled, and water cascaded down from the skies. Giant puddles reflected the lightning's glare. As the storm continued, Sir Robert and Max drifted off to sleep, but I lay awake.

Suddenly in the distance I heard hoofbeats. I twisted in my hammock, staring into the rain-spattered darkness, waiting for the next flash. When it came, I saw a horse and rider, pounding wildly along from the direction of Wynd-hamshire, heading toward the mountains and my country. Something about this rider's desperate pace filled me with panic.

As he drew close to us, his hoofbeats slowed. Another flash showed he was wearing a large-brimmed hat that hid his features. He reined up beside our carriage.

I took in a trembling breath and was about to cry out for Sir Robert when suddenly the rider shouted to his horse and was off. He still headed toward the mountains, riding through the slashing rain.

The next morning we were on our way again. It was Jane's turn to ride with Sir Robert on the driver's bench. Max was inside the carriage, and Alinor and I were riding our two horses.

"Denis," said Alinor, "could you write a letter for me?"

I looked at her in surprise. "Don't you want to do it yourself?"

She smiled. "I can't write."

"You can't?"

"I thought you knew that. No, I never learned. Girls don't do that kind of thing."

"Well, they should."

"I know. You'll have to teach me someday. But," and she looked around to make sure no one could overhear, "I want to dictate a letter to Grandpa."

"Sure," I agreed. "Sir Robert says there's an inn a mile or two ahead. We'll find a table, and I'll write it while the others are getting supplies."

The inn turned out to be a small wayside hut with no carriage repair service, much to Max's disgust. But there did happen to be a table inside, so I took off my backpack, sat down, and prepared my writing supplies. In the pack I always carried not only my leatherbound journal, but also an ink bottle and a good supply of oriental paper.

Alinor appeared beside me. "Denis, I can't find it."

I looked up. "Can't find what?"

"Oh," she said, flustered, "I forgot. You don't know about it."

"What're you talking about?"

"Sorry," she sighed, and sat down on a chair beside me. "There's so much to keep in mind these days. It takes all my energy just trying to keep straight who I can tell what to. Sometimes I get sick of this whole mess, all this secrecy."

"I'll bet you do," I sympathized. "What did you lose?"

"My seal."

"Your seal? You mean, like for a letter?"

"Yes. It's a royal seal."

I leaped from my chair. "What," I whispered tensely, glancing around, "are you doing with a royal seal? I know you're a princess, but what if someone finds it?"

Alinor looked at me meditatively. "Sometimes I don't like you, Denis."

I felt as though I'd been slugged by Max. "Why not?"

"Who do you think you are, anyway? My father?"

I bit my lip and was silent.

"Answer me! Sometimes you act like my keeper."

"Hey, listen," I said as calmly as I could, "you've played mommy to me enough times the last couple weeks—I guess I can play daddy to you once in a while."

Two hot red spots appeared in her fair cheeks. Her eyes smoldered. "Denis Anwyck—"

"Anything for lunch today?" boomed the voice of the innkeeper behind us. We both jumped, and in spite of ourselves burst into nervous laughter.

"No, thanks," I said hastily. "Not unless you want anything, Alinor."

"No. Nothing."

"Sorry," I said when he'd gone. "I apologize."

"Don't. It's my fault for being so jumpy. Especially when I've lost the seal."

"Where did you last see it?"

"I don't know." She seemed almost ready to cry. "I can't remember when I used it last."

"Wow," I breathed.

"I know. It was my father's seal. It had his name and coat of arms on it." She sighed again. "I was going to use it on the letter I want to send to Grandpa. When there's a royal seal on the letter it goes more quickly and safely. But I guess there's no sense in dictating one now."

I frowned thoughtfully. "Boy, we'd better find that seal. You checked the carriage?"

"It's not there. It's not in my things or in Jane's things. I don't even remember packing it."

"Could somebody have stolen it while you were still back at the town house?"

"That's what's been worrying me."

"Do you think the baron might have found it?"

She nodded. "I think he found it, and that's how he discovered who I am."

Back on the road we were more watchful. When Jane and Max weren't around, Alinor told Sir Robert about the seal. He suggested that Alinor always ride Angel rather than taking a turn in the carriage. That way, if we were ambushed, she'd have a better chance of escaping.

"Ouch." Alinor winced. "I'm not sure I like the idea of a whole day of sidesaddle riding. But I'll hold out as long as I can."

As our journey resumed, I rode beside her. She told me more about her father, Prince Geoffrey.

"I remember being naughty," she said, "many times."

"Ah, come on," I grinned. "I'll bet you were a perfect kid."

She shook her head and smiled wryly. "How do you think I was able to sneak out of a tightly locked town house without the servants or a light sleeper like the baroness knowing? It was my favorite trick back home in Wyndhamshire. My dad and mom and I lived in a huge mansion, and he always had it locked up tight. But I knew my way out—and back in again."

I glanced at her sideways. From the very first time I saw her, a month ago in Charles's woodworking shop when she came to pick up a wooden chest for the baroness, she had seemed like a girl who could take care of herself.

"But the funny thing is," she continued, "I don't remember him ever spanking me. Daddy was like Grandpa. He was never irritated with me, just deeply grieved when I was bad. And when I saw how much my behavior hurt him, it was 10 times worse than any spanking ever could be."

A muffled "Yahoo!" came to us from up ahead. Jane had jumped nimbly from the driver's bench beside Sir Robert, landed on the dusty road, and was now running back toward us.

"That's quite a companion you've got," I murmured to Alinor.

"You're telling me," she said.

"My turn, Denis," Jane gasped as she arrived beside my stallion.

"OK," I agreed cheerfully, and slid off one side while she scrambled up the other.

I jogged ahead to the carriage and joined Max inside.

"Look at this."

"What?"

"This piece of the old underbrace." He held out the broken shaft of wood.

I looked at it closely. "What about it?"

"Use your eyes, Denis."

I turned the piece over and over. "It's broken. But we both knew that already."

He ran his finger along one side of the break. "See this?"

"You mean that straight edge?"

"Yeah." He took the wood and sighted along the crack. "We were sabotaged."

I stared at him.

"Somebody," he continued, "took a thin saw or a sharp knife and sliced this partway through."

Ice formed down my spine. "When?"

He shrugged. "Beats me. But it had to have been after the king decided to take our carriage."

"Max," I said, "do you realize what this means?"

"Yeah," he said solemnly. "It means that one of the baron's assistants—maybe one of his knights—is on our trail."

"Why? If the brace were cut back home, why would we be in danger here?"

"Don't you get it? A break like this couldn't hurt us by itself—we can't go fast enough to roll over or anything like that. No," he said, "whoever cut this brace is probably trailing us, waiting for us to break down."

"And when it did break, you fixed it so fast that we were back on the road in no time."

"Right." He slid open the rear window of the carriage. We looked out to where the girls were riding, and then past them down the long, dusty road. "But whoever's on our trail may not be that far behind."

CHAPTER

s soon as we took a rest stop, Max showed Sir
Robert the slit in the broken underbrace. The
knight looked grim. "Check the other one," he
said.

Max's eyes grew wide. "I hadn't thought of that." He
rolled under the carriage. "The other one's cut too."

Sir Robert looked around uneasily. "Will it hold?"

"It should be OK as long as we don't go too fast. But,"
added Max, "this time I don't have a spare."

"So if this one breaks," I said, "we're sitting ducks."

"Right."

That night Sir Robert guided the wagon into a grove of
trees. We cooked supper over a tiny, shielded campfire.

"We are in very serious danger," Sir Robert said when
we'd finished eating and stamped out the fire. He told the
girls about the discovery of the other sabotaged underbrace. "And," he continued, "I think it's high time that
everybody knows exactly why we're going on this trip.
That way we'll all recognize the seriousness of keeping
alert."

In the chill twilight I could see the two girls huddle
closer together.

"First of all," the knight continued, "I think that Max
and Jane should know Alinor's true identity."

Alinor caught her breath.

"Alinor," said Sir Robert, "is the crown princess. The king is her grandfather, and she is next in line to the throne."

Max hiccuped. Jane scrambled away from Alinor and knelt at a respectful distance.

Alinor burst into tears. "Oh, Sir Robert, now you've ruined everything," she sobbed. "Jane, please! Please, come back here."

"I'd—I'd rather not, Your Highness," said Jane meekly.

"And quit calling me Your Highness," Alinor said desperately. "I'm not any more of a highness than you are. I already told you you didn't have to call me 'Miss Alinor.' Please forget all that and come back and sit with me."

Jane hesitated. "I better not."

"Jane," said Alinor in a heartbreaking voice, "you're the only girlfriend I've got. Please. I'm just a scared 13-year-old kid."

We waited in the semidarkness while Jane struggled with her shyness.

"OK," she finally said, and scooted over to sit beside Alinor again. Alinor embraced her gratefully.

Sir Robert cleared his throat. "Thank you, Jane," he said. "Now, I need to tell you something that even Alinor doesn't know. Alinor, we had hoped to keep this from you. On the day of Denis's investiture, you may have seen the Wyndhamshire knight enter the courtyard."

"I saw him. He came to declare war, didn't he? I knew that."

"That he did," said Sir Robert. "But that isn't all he told us. He told us, Alinor, that your father, Prince Geoffrey, has been accused of murdering Prince Andrew of Wyndhamshire."

Alinor gasped in horror. "That's a lie!"

"I'm sure it is," said Sir Robert calmly. "But—"

"My father was not a murderer!"

"I knew your father very well," Sir Robert reminded her, "and I totally agree. But what is important is that the king of Wyndhamshire believes he was."

"He couldn't possibly believe it," wailed Alinor. "Not him! He and Grandpa are best friends. Dad was like another son to him. Anyway," she said indignantly, "how could Daddy be a murderer? He was the one who got killed!"

"I don't know all the details."

"Who's behind this? Is it the baron?"

"That's what I'm thinking," said Sir Robert. "But the important thing to remember is that whether or not it's true, the people in the palace at Wyndhamshire believe it. And that is why we are in grave danger. Someone is following us."

"Would it be better if we went back home?" I suggested. "We could come back again with a military escort."

Sir Robert was silent for a while. Then he said, "No. It's tempting, but since we're already this far along, we may as well keep going. For one thing, the carriage couldn't make it back over the mountains. My guess is that our pursuers are following several miles back. They're assuming the carriage will break down—and even if it doesn't, they think we're going directly to the king's palace. If we can get to the Bock farm before they catch up, we'll hide the carriage in the barn and they'll never know where we went."

That night we began posting a watch. Using the moon as a clock, Sir Robert stood guard first. After it rose to a certain point, he woke me, and after I'd stood guard a few hours, I woke Max.

The next morning Sir Robert, who'd exchanged his knightly robes for those of a peasant farmer, took the reins. "You boys try to get some sleep," he urged us.

So we climbed into the hammock bunks inside the carriage. Max dropped off right away, emitting feeble snores. But even though my eyes were tired, my brain was wide awake. And it didn't help matters that the girls, who were on horseback, had left their mounts tied to the rear corners of the wagon. I could hear everything they said perfectly. What I heard convinced me that it hadn't taken Jane long to get over her shyness at Alinor's being a princess.

"Have you ever met Arnold?" she asked Alinor.

"Arnold who?"

"Arnold," said Jane. "The butcher's son. Everybody knows Arnold."

"I don't," Alinor said glumly. Sir Robert's revelations last night had put her in a somber mood.

"Arnold's my boyfriend."

"Oh?"

"Yeah," Jane said enthusiastically. "I'm going to marry him next summer."

"Aren't you too young?"

"No, I'm not too young," Jane declared. "Anyway, he's 17."

"And you're 12."

"Twelve and a half," Jane corrected.

Alinor made a disgusted sound with her tongue. "And his parents gave him permission to marry you?"

"Well," Jane admitted, "it's actually not settled yet. I have to work out a few details."

"Like what?"

"Like, maybe, asking Arnold."

Alinor laughed unpleasantly. "You haven't even asked Arnold yet?"

"Not yet," Jane confessed. "In fact, we've actually talked only a couple times—once when I was walking by his shop, and the other time when the baroness sent me to get some meat for Marie, that same afternoon I met you."

"But you're still pretty sure you're getting married in the summer." There was quite a bit of acid in Alinor's tone. I tried to ignore their conversation and drift off to sleep. Then Jane switched topics again.

"Your Highness, do you have a boyfriend?"

"Jane, what did I tell you last night?" Alinor snapped. "Don't call me that."

"Sorry." Jane paused. "Do you have a boyfriend, Alinor?"

"That's better."

"Do you?"

"Do I *what*?"

"Have a boyfriend?"

There was a deadly pause. My stomach tightened, ready for a sarcastic reply. But to my surprise, Alinor's next words were calm. "Jane," she said casually, "what kind of stores would you like to visit when we get to Wyndhamshire?"

"I'll bet Sir Robert and Denis and Max won't let us go shopping. Sounds like it's too dangerous. I like Max," she said, getting back to her preferred subject.

"I thought you liked what's-his-name, Ambrose."

"*Arnold*. Yeah, he's OK. But I like Max just as much. Max works for his dad, doesn't he?"

"I believe so," said Alinor wearily.

"I wonder how much he makes."

"You mean money? He's just an apprentice."

"But he'll inherit his dad's business, won't he?" asked Jane anxiously.

"Probably."

"Alinor," Jane asked, then paused. "Do you like Denis?"

10

I quickly put my fingers into my ears and began to hum loudly and nervously. I didn't want to hear Alinor's response, whatever it was.

That stupid Jane. After a few seconds I cautiously unplugged one ear.

"I like Denis," Jane was saying. The skinny little mophead apparently loved the whole world. How touching. "I wonder," she continued, "how much money he makes at the castle."

"Jane, that's really none of your business," Alinor said in a voice that lowered the temperature 20 degrees.

"Has Denis ever proposed to you?"

"Don't be silly!" Alinor sputtered.

"I like Denis." Jane sighed. "I like the way his hair sort of curls up near his neck. I'd like to run my fingers through it."

I jabbed my fingers back into my ears so quickly that I think I cut one of them with my fingernail. I scrunched up in the hammock and kept my ears plugged for so long that I guess I fell asleep.

I was awakened by the jolting of the carriage. Max, in the upper hammock, woke up too. "Hey," he said groggily, "we shouldn't be going over rough ground like this. That underbrace—"

The carriage creaked to a stop. I heard a couple of

chickens cackling close by, and the mooing of a cow.

"I'll bet we're at the Bocks'," I said, and rolled out of my hammock and hit the floor. Max scrambled down beside me. Smoothing down our hair as best we could, we emerged from the carriage.

Blinking in the sunlight, we stared around us. We'd arrived at a tiny farm. Sir Robert had parked the carriage behind a cozy cottage. A large barn loomed above us on a nearby rise of ground; a few milk cows gazed at us with mild curiosity. The two girls had dismounted, and as a group we walked with them around the cottage to the front.

As we approached the door, it opened. A tall, severe-looking woman stepped quickly out, carrying a cloth bag. The white locks of her hair burst wildly from her head. She glanced at Sir Robert's peasant costume without interest. Putting her head back inside the doorway for a moment she called in a deep and powerful voice, "Goodbye, Mrs. Bock. Please call me again if you need me. By the way, you have visitors. Peddlers, I think." Leaving the door ajar, she stalked quickly down the drive and was soon out of sight.

Mrs. Bock, who now appeared in the doorway, was far different from the first woman. She was small and plump, with soft gray hair. Her reddened eyes and flushed faced told us she had been crying.

"Yes?" she said, looking first at Sir Robert and then at the rest of us. "What can I do for you?"

Sir Robert smiled disarmingly. "Mrs. Bock," he said, "you may not recognize me because of my clothing, but I am Sir Robert, a friend of Prince Geoffrey. I hope my messenger reached you. I bring you greetings from the prince's father."

Mrs. Bock stared at us, and as she did so her face melted again into tears. She slumped against the doorway, sobbing bitterly. Alinor instinctively went to her and put her arm around her.

"Thank you," sobbed Mrs. Bock, "thank you, sweet thing. Forgive me. It's just so sad . . . Please, come in, won't you?"

We followed her inside. She motioned to us to sit down around an old table next to the fireplace. "Forgive me," she said again, "but I haven't been the same since my husband died."

Sir Robert glanced up quickly. "Mr. Bock is dead?"

"Yes," she said mournfully. "He passed to his rest last week. We buried him yesterday."

"I am so sorry," said Sir Robert sympathetically. Then he asked quickly, "How are you fixed financially? His Majesty my king will wish to assist you, if you need it."

She shook her head. "I'm doing pretty well. I plan to sell the farm and go live with my sister and her husband in Wyndhamshire. I'm going to be quite comfortable. But it just won't be the same without him."

"This is a tragedy," murmured Sir Robert. "Had he been ill long?"

"Not long," she said. "Just a few days. He took sick and the doctor tried her best, but she wasn't able to save him. I think it was his heart."

"She? The doctor is a woman?"

"Yes. Dr. Skotia, the woman who just left us a moment ago. She is court physician to the king of Wyndhamshire. A natural healer she is, and though many do not accept her as a doctor because she is female, she has done much good."

"I remember the doctor vaguely from when I lived back in Wyndhamshire," Alinor said thoughtfully. "But nobody saw much of her. And I heard rumors that she wasn't always in her right mind."

"Yes, she has had her problems. I know her well." Mrs. Bock suddenly stirred and rose to her feet. "But I am forgetting. You've been traveling. You are hungry."

"Don't worry about us," Sir Robert assured her.

"No," said Mrs. Bock firmly. "No more talking until I get a good meal into you." She looked at the two girls hesitantly. "I wonder if I might take the liberty of asking your ladyships to help me with one or two things."

"Sure," Jane said. She jumped up, her eyes twinkling with the novelty of being called a lady. "Come on, Alinor." And soon the three of them were chattering together, slicing things and putting them into a pan over the hearth.

Max, looking around for something to do, discovered a broken chair in the corner, and set about trying to fix it.

"Denis, would you assemble your writing materials," asked Sir Robert. "I want to dictate a document to the Wyndhamshire king."

Supper was ready before we knew it, and when the document was done, we gathered again around the cozy table. Several candles cast a warm circle of light on our faces. Glancing at Alinor and Mrs. Bock, I could see that both seemed much happier.

I was glad to notice the expression on Alinor's face—it was like the one she used to wear before all this had happened. It was a courageous, almost daredevil expression, as though she were ready for anything—and ready to do anything to see good triumph.

"And now, Sir Robert," said Mrs. Bock when supper was over, "you wish to stay here while in Wyndhamshire?"

"Yes. But will we be too many for you?"

"Denis and I can sleep in the carriage," Max offered.

"That would probably help," Mrs. Bock admitted. "But by all means, you all must stay here at the farm."

"The king has authorized us to reward you handsomely for your services," Sir Robert told her.

"And," Max said, "I'm a woodworker's apprentice, so I can do any repairs you need around the farm."

"And we'll help clean house," offered Alinor.

"I'll chop wood," I said.

"That would be helpful," Mrs. Bock said eagerly. "There is much to be done, especially since—"

"I know," Sir Robert interrupted sympathetically. He paused, then continued. "There is one more thing I must ask you."

"Yes?"

"Can you tell us anything about the recent trouble between Wyndhamshire and our country?"

"What do you mean?"

Sir Robert leaned forward. "I am interested in how the trouble began. We always thought there was such a good relationship between our two countries. Our kings were such great friends."

Mrs. Bock was silent for awhile.

"Are you sworn to secrecy?" the knight asked.

"In a way, yes," she said. "My husband urged me never to tell anyone what he had told me, probably because he feared for my safety. But I feel since he's gone, and since there's so much trouble that you may be able to help, perhaps my vow need no longer be kept."

"Did it have to do with the start of the rumors about Prince Geoffrey?"

Mrs. Bock looked at us gravely. "I'm sorry to have to say this, but they were not rumors."

Alinor stared at her. "Not rumors? About my father?"

It was Mrs. Bock's turn to stare. "Your father?"

"I am Princess Alinor."

Mrs. Bock's mouth dropped open. Her eyes darted quickly to Sir Robert's.

He nodded soberly. "This is the crown princess."

"I'm afraid, Your Highness," said Mrs. Bock in a trembling voice, "that just before he died, your father did a very, very terrible thing."

11

In the glow of the candles Alinor's face was chalk-white.

"No," she said fiercely.

Mrs. Bock reached over and patted her hand. "Perhaps I should say nothing right now."

"Go ahead and tell me," Alinor said. "But it's a lie."

Mrs. Bock glanced at Sir Robert.

"You may as well tell us what you know," he said quietly.

Mrs. Bock sighed. "I never would have believed it if my own husband hadn't been right there. As you know, Prince Andrew and Prince Geoffrey were the closest of friends. Geoffrey had been introducing the ideas of his father, and Andrew stood by his side. Finally it seemed that Andrew's father was accepting these ideas. He actually moved out of his castle and began to live in an old palace in the city.

"Then, about a year ago, a rumor was whispered around the palace that Prince Geoffrey had accused Andrew of some terrible crime. The king could scarcely believe this, but he still had enough old-school chivalry in his veins to demand that Andrew and Geoffrey meet so that Andrew could defend his honor.

"Geoffrey steadily denied the rumor, and perhaps Andrew believed him, but nobody else did. Finally the two princes agreed to meet one night in the palace garden. Both insisted that no one else be present, and their wish was granted.

"My husband, as Geoffrey's squire, waited outside the garden wall. He was alone because Andrew's squire was ill. The princes both gave their swords to him and took a torch with them to light their way."

Mrs. Bock sighed. "Suddenly in the darkness Geoffrey stood close by my husband and said urgently, 'Bock, my sword!' My husband reluctantly handed over the sword, saying, 'Then take Prince Andrew's also.' Geoffrey said 'No, just mine.' So my husband gave him the sword, and a short time later there were dreadful cries in the darkness. Mr. Bock rushed into the garden, found the nearly-extinguished torch lying on the ground, blew it into life again, and held it high. By its light he saw both princes lying dead."

"But how could both of them be dead?" I asked. "If Prince Geoffrey was the only one with a sword—"

"Andrew had fought valiantly with all he had—a small dagger he'd drawn from a sheath at his belt. It was all he had to defend himself with," Mrs. Bock said sadly. "It's not much, of course, against a three-foot sword."

The flames crackled cheerfully in the fireplace, and the candles on the table glowed warmly. But it was as if a frozen wind from the northern mountains had entered Mrs. Bock's tiny cottage.

"It's a lie," whispered Alinor.

"Why did it come out now?" asked Sir Robert. "Why has it been kept quiet for a year?"

"My husband kept it quiet," Mrs. Bock said simply. "When he found the two princes lying dead, he quickly wiped the dagger and replaced it in its sheath on Andrew's belt. Then he bloodied Andrew's sword and placed it in his hand so as to make it appear that there was a fair fight."

"So your husband just recently revealed what he

knew?" Sir Robert asked her.

"Yes," she said somberly, "just before he died. He wanted to clear his heart, so he told what he knew to Dr. Skotia and me."

"The woman doctor we saw when we came?"

"Yes."

"And Dr. Skotia told the king?"

"Yes. As the palace physician, she naturally went immediately to His Majesty."

"So she's responsible for the war," Max said.

"No," said Mrs. Bock regretfully. "Prince Geoffrey is responsible."

"It's a lie," repeated Alinor tensely.

"Are you sure that you still wish us to use your cottage as our base?" Sir Robert asked Mrs. Bock.

"Please do," she said earnestly. "For as long as you wish."

The next morning Sir Robert and I mounted the two carriage horses, ready to leave for the king's palace. We'd both thrown peasants' cloaks over our court garments.

"I'm sorry you can't ride your stallion," he apologized, "but people would immediately be suspicious if they saw two peasants riding such fine horses."

Alinor appeared in the doorway, dressed for travel. Her eyes burned brightly above sallow cheeks. She looked as though she hadn't slept at all. "I'm coming with you," she announced.

Sir Robert respectfully shook his head. "No."

"Yes. I'll ride behind Denis."

"No, Alinor," said Sir Robert.

"Why not?"

"If you come with us simply as a noble girl, you will arouse curiosity in the palace as to why a noble girl would accompany a diplomat and his scribe. And obviously you can't go as Princess Alinor."

"I'm coming with you," she repeated. "If Max can go into town to visit the woodworking shops, I can come with you."

"Max is different," said the knight. "He is a private citizen. And even if you tried to keep your identity secret, what if someone at the palace recognized you as Prince Geoffrey's daughter? You might be taken hostage and imprisoned."

"But we're in the Fortnight of Peace. No one will harm me."

"I once believed that," said Sir Robert sadly. "But evil things are happening here, and I don't trust treaties or people any more."

"My father did not murder Prince Andrew."

"I am sure he did not. But many people here believe that he did. And that's the situation we have to work with."

Alinor walked toward my horse. "Give me your hand, Denis."

"You are staying, Princess," Sir Robert said gently. "You can do nothing to help. Your grandfather has lost a son. I refuse to let him lose a granddaughter as well."

Alinor was silent for a moment. "Then at least let Jane and me go shopping. We can both ride Angel."

Sir Robert paused.

I said, "Max is going into town anyway, Sir Robert. The girls could go with him."

He nodded. "As long as they're simply tourists and no one knows where they're from, I suppose it's all right." He glanced around him. "Under the terms of the Fortnight of Peace, the common people—the ones you'd meet in the shops—aren't supposed to be told about the war yet. And it looks like that part of the treaty is holding. I haven't noticed any preparations for battle."

He turned to Alinor. "Yes. You may go to town with

Jane. But you must return before evening. And you must not go near the palace."

She raised her chin rebelliously. "I want to see the graves of my parents. They are buried next to the palace."

Sir Robert shook his head emphatically. "You must wait to visit their grave until someone is with you. Perhaps tomorrow."

Sir Robert and I rode through a pasture behind the barn and out a distant gate. Skirting the edge of nearby Ashton, we wended our way through several meadows before reaching the highroad that led to the city of Wyndhamshire.

"We want to make it almost impossible for anyone to connect the king's diplomatic mission with the Bock farm," Sir Robert explained to me. "That way, it can always be a safe haven for us—and if we have to escape it will be easier from there."

The city of Wyndhamshire, which, as I mentioned earlier, was the capital of the country of the same name, stood just a couple miles from Ashton, where the Bock farm was.

"What's that?" I asked.

"Where?"

"Up ahead." I pointed forward along the straight, level highroad where a large group of people approached us.

"Very interesting," murmured Sir Robert.

"It looks like they're carrying spears."

"Not spears," said Sir Robert. "Something else."

"Shovels," I said, when we'd come a little closer. "Picks and shovels and hoes."

"I can't understand it," said the knight. "There must be 300 men in that crowd."

"Couldn't it just be a group of farm workers heading out for the field?"

"No, not that large a group. Anyway, if they were

farmers they'd be carrying scythes and grain sacks. This is harvesttime, not planting time."

Soon we reached the mob, and as we threaded our way through them we heard the word "river" several times. Once they'd passed, Sir Robert looked grave.

"So that's what they're doing."

"What do you mean?"

"From the little I heard, there can be no doubt where they're going and what they're going to do when they get there. They're traveling to the border to reroute the river so it won't flow through our country. It means a famine in our land next year. It's the first step in a siege."

12

After Sir Robert had removed his peasant's cloak and placed it in his saddlebag, he and I rode quickly along the great avenue that led to the royal residence. As we approached the huge, ivy-covered palace, I noticed a tall wrought-iron fence enclosing a sort of park. A closely-planted line of trees stood just beyond the fence, and through their branches I could see stone monuments.

"The cemetery?" I asked.

"Yes." The knight glanced around uneasily. "One of these days when it's safe I'll try to get Alinor in there. But I don't like the way things are going, Denis. Not one bit."

We arrived at a large carved iron gate that stood in front of the palace. Through the metalwork we could see a young page boy seated on a stool. One of our horses snuffled, and the boy jumped to his feet.

"May I help you, sirs?" he asked.

Sir Robert dismounted and explained who he was. He handed the page the document I had written for him the night before. "Please take this to someone who will give it to your king," he directed.

The boy was gone for about 15 minutes. When he returned, his face was watchful. "Come in."

He opened the gate and we rode through. Sir Robert muttered something under his breath. The boy led us down a long brick walkway to the palace doors. "Tie your horses to that tree," he said, "then follow me."

Sir Robert and I dismounted and tied our horses. Then the knight suddenly turned on the boy. "Where are the hostlers?"

"Sir?"

"The stablehands? Where are they? Why aren't they caring for our mounts?"

The boy gazed at him steadily. "Please follow me," he said.

Walking beside Sir Robert, I could sense the knight's intense rage, but I didn't quite understand it.

"In here, please," said the boy, and gestured us through a side doorway. The room we entered was small and unfurnished except for a long bench under one window. "Have a seat," said the page, and disappeared.

Alone, Sir Robert began to confide in me. "It's not that I mind how they treat *me*," he said, "but we're on a diplomatic mission, representing our king. They've shown us nothing but the deepest disrespect."

He stared frostily around the room. "Under normal circumstances, that document would have gained us instant respect. The page would have showered us with 'yes, sirs' and 'if you please, sirs.' He would have brought a knight along with him, and several hostlers. The hostlers would have taken our horses to the best stables, and the knight would have led us to a comfortable chamber to wait, rather than this—this storeroom."

"What does it mean?"

"It means," said Sir Robert, "that His Majesty the king of Wyndhamshire is gravely offended. And it means that if we make the slightest slip we will probably be taken prisoners and our lives might even be in danger."

We were silent for a while.

"Promise me one thing, Denis," he said. "If we get out

of here alive, please keep a close watch on Alinor."

"I'll do my best, Sir Robert."

"She's not thinking clearly now. Her emotions make her very dangerous."

"And," I added, "she doesn't realize how deeply offended the Wyndhamshire king is."

"Exactly. So I urge you, once we're out of here go with her wherever she goes. Don't let her out of your sight."

I nodded doubtfully. I wasn't sure how Alinor was going to like my being her constant companion.

"Where is everybody?" Sir Robert fumed. He sneezed violently. "It's dusty in here."

After nearly an hour, the door finally opened, admitting a tall woman. I stared at her. Where had I seen her before?

Then I remembered. She was the doctor we'd seen leaving the Bock farm. As before, her unruly white hair burst from her head in wild, separate locks. She had about her the faint odor of musty herbs.

"Sir Robert?" she asked in her deep, cracked voice.

The knight rose to his feet. I stood too. "I am Sir Robert. This is my scribe, Squire Denis Anwyck."

She smiled briefly. She did not appear to recognize us. "I am Dr. Skotia. I understand you wish to see His Majesty."

"We do."

"I am afraid it is impossible today."

Sir Robert took a long breath. "I am afraid I must insist."

"It will do you no good," she replied.

"And why not?"

"The king has sent me to relay word to you that in order to express his deep outrage at the cold-blooded murder of his son by Prince Geoffrey he will not see you

until tomorrow. And then he will see you alone, without your scribe."

Sir Robert looked as though someone had slapped him across the face. "There has been a dreadful mistake."

"What mistake?"

"About Prince Andrew's death."

"The facts are clear."

"Prince Geoffrey was not the kind of man to do what you describe."

"My king believes he was," said the doctor. "Geoffrey's own squire, Bock, told me so with his own lips, a few days before his death."

"Bock may have been lying, or at least in error."

"It's hardly likely he was lying," she replied drily. "From long experience I have found that a man on his deathbed realizes that he has no more reason to lie. He almost always tells the truth."

"The truth as he sees it."

The doctor raised her eyebrows. "I suppose you are right," she murmured. "The truth as he sees it."

As a final indignity, the page boy led us around to the servant's entrance at the back and let us out through the gate there.

"I feel so helpless, Denis," growled Sir Robert as we rode back along the avenue. "I have never experienced anything like this in all my diplomatic service. The real tragedy isn't the war or the rerouting of the river. It's the enmity between two very friendly peoples."

We turned into the town's main square.

"Shall I find Max and the girls?" I asked.

He nodded. "Yes, find them and bring them back to the farm as soon as you can. Remember to take the back roads."

"Where are you going?"

"I'm going back to the farm to do some thinking. Come as soon as you can."

Fortunately, it was easy to find Jane and Alinor. In these big towns stores are arranged together according to what they sell—all the clothing stores on one street, all the woodworking shops were on another, and so on. So I simply trotted to the clothiers' district, and soon I saw the girls, carrying two large bundles, emerge from a shop. They were mounting Angel as I rode up.

"Hi, Denis," said Alinor. She was smiling and looked in a better mood than she had for days.

"Hi," I answered. "Have a good time shopping?"

"Yeah." Jane's brown eyes shone. "Thanks to Alinor."

"Sorry to have to cut your shopping short," I said apologetically, "but Sir Robert wants us back at the Bock farm right away. Things have gone terribly wrong at the palace."

Alinor's eyes widened. "What do you mean?"

After making sure no one could overhear, I quickly told them what had happened. Alinor's smile vanished, and her eyes became large and tragic.

"It's the end of the world," she whispered sadly.

"Maybe not," I said, trying to sound confident. "Sir Robert's heading back to the Bock farm to sketch out some new ideas. Come and help me find Max, and then we'll head back."

Alinor grimaced. "We were just going to the pastry shop. Could you pick us up there when you find him? And if we're not there, we'll be in that store right next door."

I thought a moment. I'd secretly been hoping to spend some time in a bookstore I'd noticed just around the corner. I could stop there quickly before I found Max.

"OK," I agreed, "but you two stick together. I'll be back as soon as I can."

CHAPTER

13

The bookstore was everything I'd hoped it would be. I emerged a quarter of an hour later, having bought a volume on history and another on speedwriting.

I galloped down to the woodworkers' street, tied my stallion to a hitching-ring, and peered into the shops, one by one. In one of the larger ones I found Max in conversation with a bunch of teenage apprentices; the latter had taken advantage of the absence of the owner by gathering around a counter to chat. I drifted in and stood on the edge of the group.

It was clear that the apprentices were doing their best to tell Max about life in the big city. A red-faced boy had the floor at the moment. "And then," he chuckled, "she asked me, 'How much does this cost?' "

The others waited, eyes shining.

"Now keep in mind," said the red-faced boy, "15 minutes earlier I'd just sold this exact style of wooden handkerchief box to another woman for two shillings, right? Well, I took one look at this new customer and I saw that she wasn't from around here at all, you know what I mean? She was a country bumpkin, right? Like Max here."

The others roared with laughter. Max flushed, but tried to keep a grin on his face.

"She had country lassie written all over her. I said to

myself, 'But she's a rich country lassie.' Are you a rich country lassie, Max?"

"Get to the point, Rupert," said an impatient listener.

"So I got my courage up," continued Rupert, "and I said in my smoothest-most-aristocratic voice, 'Madam,' I said, 'I wouldn't tell this to everyone, but the very box you hold in your hand was actually made by order of Prince Andrew. The day before he was killed in the duel he ordered it for the princess.' I could say this, you see, because this woman was from somewhere way out in the boonies where she didn't even know that Prince Andrew was a bachelor."

"You dirty dog," someone said, "taking advantage of a poor country girl!"

"Poor nothing," retorted Rupert. "She was definitely not poor. Well, when she heard that, her eyes got as big as dinner plates. 'Reee-lly?' she said. Just like that. 'Reee-lly? How do I know that's true?' "

"So," said another boy, "she wasn't a sucker like you thought, right?"

"Wait!" Rupert held up a restraining hand. "I'm not done yet. I put on a really sober face and said, 'Madam, I am surprised that you doubt me. Isn't this his very own coat of arms on the lid?' "

"Rupert! You didn't tell her that."

"Sure, I did. And what's so funny is that the carved design on the top really wasn't a coat of arms at all. Let me show you." He reached under the counter and brought out a small wooden box.

"We had 30 or 40 of these just under the counter. And you know how we always polish one of them really good as a sample, and then switch it at the last minute before we pack it? The sample was the one I showed her—but she thought it was the only one of its kind. Look at the design on the top. Just three flowers and a bird. But you should have heard me go on about it."

"What did you tell her?"

"I did like this." Rupert bent reverently over the box and pointed to one of the flowers. " 'Madam, Prince Andrew explained his coat of arms to me so that we could carve it correctly. Do you see this flower on the right? That flower is a lily, and signifies peace.' And she said, 'Oh, how beautiful.' "

The other boys roared. Max giggled.

" 'And madam, do you see this beautiful rose on the left? Prince Andrew told me that it stands for joy. And this lovely bluebell in the center stands for love, madam, the love that Prince Andrew had for his lady fair.' "

Several of the boys were choking with laughter and gasping for air. "How much? How much did you get for it? Did she buy it?"

Rupert's eyebrows rose. "Of course she bought it! How could she resist? I told her, 'Madam, my feelings for my slain prince are so deep that I am reluctant to sell it at any price.' She pleaded with me to sell it to her. She offered me 20 shillings, then 40. When she got to 100 I finally said, 'Madam, if this humble work of art can gladden your home—if the beautiful flowers on its lid can indeed bring peace and joy and love to your own marriage, I will allow you to take it with you. But in memory of my prince, I must ask you for 150 shillings. I must also tell you that most of that money will be donated to the prince's favorite charity.' "

"Rupert, you dog. Did she bite?"

"She bit," said Rupert deliciously. "One hundred and fifty silver shillings, and a bonus of 10 shillings to me for making it available to her."

Max asked, "What did your dad say?"

"Dad?" Rupert giggled. "Dad wasn't around. He'd gone to replace a blade on a carving knife. I was the only one in the shop, just like today."

"I mean, what did your dad say when he got back?"

Rupert snorted. "Do you think I was stupid enough to tell him?"

Max gulped. "You kept all the money for yourself?"

"All but a couple of shillings. I just told Dad I'd sold another box, gave him two shillings, and that was that."

"What did you do with the rest of it?" Max asked.

"Part of it went for this." After looking carefully around, he reached beneath his shirt and pulled out a beautiful jeweled dagger on the end of a neck chain. "See? It just fits my hand. It's got a five-inch blade, which'll go in as far as the heart, and then some."

"What would your dad do to you if he knew how you suckered that girl?"

"Whip me, probably. But Dad has no room to talk. I've seen him pull some fast ones in his time. See that rocking chair?"

We glanced across the room at a highly polished rocker.

"Beautiful, right? Solid? Good workmanship?"

We nodded.

"But Dad won't sell it to local people. If he did, they'd be in here six months later screaming for their money back. This chair just doesn't hold up. It's OK when you try it out in the shop. It's OK for a few months, especially if you don't let kids jump on it. But it won't last more than half a year. That's why it's good for tourists. Rich tourists."

"Why don't you make it solid in the first place?" Max asked hesitantly.

Rupert looked at him for a long moment. "Boy, you are a country cousin, aren't you? I'll tell you why we don't make it solid in the first place," said Rupert frankly. "It takes too much time. Everybody wants such a bargain these days. And if it takes you two full days to make a chair, and you get only 10 shillings for it, you're not going to get rich."

Max opened his mouth. "But—"

"Another thing, six months down the line these rich people are going to redecorate their house with something entirely different. Furniture fashions change. In a year or so that chair will end up at the dump."

"But—"

"Listen, buddy," Rupert said meaningfully, his fingertip two inches from Max's nose, "you gotta make a decision. You either join the fourteenth century or go back to where you came from. You told us your dad has a little shop in some burg, right? Well, if you want to sit there squatting on a workbench 12 hours a day grinding out stodgy old furniture that'll last for centuries, then do it. I don't care. But," he continued, "while you're out there in the boonies scrimping and saving and trying to make ends meet, I'll be here in Wyndhamshire owning a town house and a country house and a cottage by the big river. My kids'll be the best-dressed kids in town. The king will knight me for my service to the nation's economy. So! What do you think of that?"

Max said nothing. But I could tell he was thinking.

Suddenly I remembered. Max and I had to join Alinor and Jane and get back to Mrs. Bock's farm. Now!

14

What a bunch of kooks," I muttered as Max and I mounted our horses outside the woodworkers' shops.

He was lashing some spare carriage underbraces to the back of his saddle. "What do you mean, kooks?"

"I'm glad to get out of there. Those guys aren't . . . clean."

"Some of what they said isn't so crazy," Max said thoughtfully.

I stared at him. "You didn't buy all that baloney, did you?"

"A lot of it makes sense."

"Like what?"

He slapped his horse to encourage it to go faster. "Where are we going?"

"Just a couple streets over. To the garment section, where I left the girls."

"Denis, don't be so quick to judge something you don't know anything about."

"I know what I want when I go into a woodworker's shop," I said. "I want quality."

"But you won't pay quality prices for it."

"I'll pay a fair price."

"What's fair?"

I snorted. "Oh, forget it. We're just flapping our

tongues. Let's get the girls and get out of here." I told him about what had happened to Sir Robert and me at the Wyndhamshire palace.

"Oh, great," he sighed. "I suppose that means we'll have to leave the country."

"What do you care?"

"I was just learning some useful principles."

I eyed him. "Something tells me your dad didn't send you over here to learn how to rook the customer."

He glared at me. "Denis, stay out of my affairs. I don't keep giving you advice about how to write, do I? Or how to squire? I just assume that you know what you need to know about squiring and I let you alone. Please do me the same courtesy."

"OK, OK," I said. "Forget I said anything."

By this time we'd entered the garment street. Arriving at the little pastry shop, I saw Jane sitting by herself on a bench just outside the door with the two bundles of dresses on her lap. She was munching on something that looked like a frosted bagel. Angel was gone too.

"Where's Alinor?" I called.

She swallowed a piece of bagel before answering. "She'll be right back. She was just going down the street to the cemetery to see her parents' graves."

I felt like someone had slugged me in the stomach. "The cemetery? She wasn't supposed to go there alone!"

"Are you sure?" Jane's face wore a puzzled frown. "She didn't act like it was a big deal or anything. She said she'd just scoot down the street and be back in a few minutes."

"How long has she been gone?"

"She left a couple of minutes ago. You just missed her."

"Here," I said frantically, "toss Max your bundles. You can ride with me." She scrambled up behind me.

"Now, the trick is not to gallop," I said to Max. "Just trot. We don't want to call attention to ourselves."

"What's going on?" Jane demanded.

"Tell you later."

It was agony to have to go so slow. Emerging from the business district, I quickened our pace a little, and soon we were in sight of the huge palace.

"Be cool," I said. "Let's just let the horses wander casually along this iron fence. The cemetery's beyond it. Keep your eyes open."

Some of the trees hid our view into the cemetery itself, but from what we could see the place looked deserted. There was no sign of either Alinor or Angel.

"She must have come and gone already," Max said. "She probably headed back another way."

I thought fast. "Max, why don't you go back to the pastry shop and wait for her. If she doesn't show up in an hour, or if Jane and I don't show up with her, then head for the farm and tell Sir Robert. Don't try to come back here."

"Yeah, but what if you get into trouble?"

"I'd rather take that risk than have Alinor sitting all by herself there on that sidewalk bench. Someone she used to know at the palace might ride by and recognize her."

Max nodded. "Good point."

Jane offered, "Maybe she headed back to the farm herself."

I shrugged my shoulders. "Who knows? Anyway, we're wasting time talking. Max, you'd better get moving."

He trotted away, and I turned to Jane. "You're sure she said she was coming here?"

"Yeah."

"She wouldn't have been planning to try to get into the palace itself, would she?"

"I doubt it. All she said was, 'I'm going to make a quick trip to the cemetery where my folks are buried. I'll be back in 10 minutes.' "

"Well, there's only one thing to do. Let's go down to the end of the street and turn the corner and see what's there."

As we rode, I squinted through the thickset trees, looking for a glint of Alinor's light blue dress. "It's an awfully big place. A lot of those markers hide our view. She could be anywhere in there." The sky gave a distant rumble. "Thunderstorm," I said. "And the wind's coming up fast. Let's hurry. Boy, I wish there was some way to know where she is."

"Wait," Jane cried. "I've got it."

"Got what?"

"Stop talking and listen." She put both index fingers between her lips and emitted a tremendously shrill whistle.

"Ouch," I yelled, massaging my right ear. "What did you do that for? That'll bring the palace guards running."

"Be still and listen."

Suddenly we heard the shrill neighing of a horse.

"Angel!" Jane breathed. "That's Alinor's signal to call her."

"But where's the horse? I can't tell. My ears are still ringing from that whistle."

"Right around that corner, like you thought," Jane replied smugly.

Throwing caution aside, we galloped to the end of the street and turned the corner. Sure enough, far up the block we saw the familiar form of Angel, tied to the railing of the cemetery fence. When she saw us she neighed again and tried to jerk free.

When we reached her, Jane slid off and patted her on the nose. Angel snorted restlessly.

"Alinor's in there somewhere," I said, dismounting.

"But how did she get through?"

Jane looked appraisingly at the iron fence. "Maybe she climbed over."

"No way. See those spikes at the top?"

"I guess you're right." She scanned the bars. "There's a gap between the bar and that stone pillar. She probably squeezed through there."

"Let's get in there."

Quickly we wriggled into the darkening cemetery. The clouds were thick and low by now, and I felt a raindrop strike my forehead. "We've got to hurry. We'll get pneumonia if we have to ride back to the Bock farm in a storm." We stepped through the line of trees and in among the gravestones. Quickly, we scrambled from row to row, scanning down the forest of granite monuments, eyes alert for a flash of blue.

A sharp cry came from somewhere close. Then a scuffling and a thump, as though something soft had fallen.

"Over there," whispered Jane. She pointed to the very edge of the markers. Half-hidden by a bush was a light-colored object. We raced along on either side of the gravestones.

Alinor lay sprawled on her back beside an open, gaping grave. A thick-shafted arrow jutted upward from her chest.

CHAPTER

15

Jane and I went down on our knees beside the prostrate Alinor. Her eyes were open, but rolled back so that only the whites were showing.

"Alinor," I sobbed, "Alinor, wake up. Don't die, Alinor." My hands trembled above the arrow.

"Leave it alone," Jane snapped. She began to tear at Alinor's clothing. Then she paused and looked up at me. "Turn your back."

"Why?" I stared at her without comprehending.

"Denis, she's not dead. She's in shock." Jane gave me a quick shove. "Turn around, unless you like to watch girls getting undressed."

"Oh," I said, and quickly turned my back. I heard the ripping of cloth. "But that arrow," I quavered. "Should I get a doctor?"

"Don't be silly." There was a pause. "It's just a flesh wound. She's lost a little blood, but not much. Take off your shirt."

"What?"

"Denis, you donkey, get your shirt off. I need bandages."

I tried to wriggle out of my shirt. In my panic it caught on my chin.

"Denis!" said Jane, exasperated. "She'll be OK. Just

tear the shirt into long strips. No, that one's too narrow. A little wider."

"Did it miss her heart?"

"The arrow? Of course, it missed her heart. But not by far. It went between her arm and her chest, and took quite a bit of skin off her arm. It may have got a little of the muscle too. Good thing it's her left side. She's right-handed."

"When will she wake up?"

"How should I know? Keep ripping bandages." Jane worked silently for a moment, then said, "There. That takes care of the blood. Now we'll try to wake her up." I heard a couple of sharp slaps.

"What are you doing?"

"Slapping her cheeks. Just relax. I know what I'm doing."

"Is she coming to?"

There was a pause. Then Jane said, "No."

"I'm getting a doctor," I said. "That woman doctor, what's-her-name."

"Stay right here. She's OK."

"Can I look at her?"

"Just a minute. There. Now she's presentable."

I turned. Alinor still lay in the same position, but now the arrow lay beside her. Her chest was covered with shreds of her dress and what was left of my shirt. Her left arm was firmly bandaged just above the elbow.

"Her eyes aren't rolling back in her head any more," I said thankfully.

"That's a good sign. Keep an eye on her, and I'll be right back." Jane darted through the gravestones to where a patch of weeds grew against the iron railings. Snatching at the heads of some of these, she hurried back. She began to rub her hands together, and soon I smelled a sharp, musty odor. "This should do it," she said. She placed her

91

open palm just beside Alinor's nose and puffed a little bit of the dust across her nostrils.

"You'll suffocate her," I protested.

"I know what I'm doing." And she did. Alinor sneezed sharply a couple of times, then opened her eyes wide. She stared at me, then at Jane, then back at me. Then pain overcame her, and her face crumpled.

"You're OK, Alinor," Jane murmured.

"What happened?" Alinor whispered. "My arm—"

Suddenly I felt a shock of fear. I'd totally forgotten that we might still be in danger. I glanced around. The rain seemed to be holding off, but the sky was even darker than before and the chill wind blew around my bare ribs. I squinted into the twilight for signs of other human beings.

"Jane, can she travel?"

Jane bit her lip. "Not by herself on a horse. She's still weak."

"But what happened?" Alinor asked faintly. "Where am I? Are we still in the—" She stopped.

I lifted the arrow into her range of vision.

She gasped. "Somebody shot me."

"Yes," I said. "Now stay calm. We've got to get you away from here."

Jane looked around fearfully, "But what if they're waiting out there for us?"

"I can't see anyone. If they wanted to kill us all they'd have had lots of opportunity to pick us off right here. I think they were just after Alinor."

"Either that or the killer got spooked when he heard us coming," Jane said.

"I'm all right," Alinor insisted, "I can ride."

"I'll hold you up," Jane said. "Let's try you on your feet."

Alinor was surprisingly steady when she stood. A thought struck me, and I reached down and picked up the arrow and thrust it into my backpack. Jane supported Alinor on one side and I on the other as we hurried toward the waiting horses.

"Denis, you go through first and toss me one of the bundles," said Jane. "And turn your back while I get her into another dress."

When the wounded girl had been reclothed, together Jane and I squeezed her through the gap in the fence. Soon we'd lifted her onto my stallion's back.

"I want Angel," she whispered.

"You can't have her," Jane said firmly. "You can't hold the reins, and I'm not good enough with a horse to handle her and you at the same time."

Soon we were off, Alinor clasping my waist. Jane rode Angel, staying as close to us as she could, watching Alinor for signs of faintness.

"You two look pretty cozy," she observed thoughtfully.

"Just for that," Alinor retorted feebly, "you've got to call me Your Highness for the rest of the week." She loosened her grasp on my waist a little. "And what are you laughing at?" she asked me.

The rain really began to pour down just as we entered Ashton. By this time Alinor felt even better—especially after Jane fed her one of Mrs. Bock's rolls from the lunch in my stallion's saddlebag. We entered the Bock farm from a side pasture and soon were in the cozy cottage.

Mrs. Bock took charge of Alinor while Sir Robert pelted me with questions. I hadn't looked forward to this interview, but I confessed everything, including my visit to the bookshop and my lingering with Max and the woodworker's apprentices. I ended with the horrible events at the graveyard. "I'm sorry, Sir Robert. I betrayed my trust."

He nodded. "You did."

"Alinor could have been killed."

He nodded again. "You didn't deserve the luck you had in finding her. I trusted you, you know."

"I'm sorry, Sir Robert."

"I know you are. But now you know how important it is to not let that girl out of your sight, don't you?"

"Yes, Sir Robert."

"Now," he said, "let's have a look at that arrow."

I handed it to him.

"A crossbow arrow," he said. "And the point still has blood on it. What a miracle it missed her heart. You say you saw no one close by."

"No one."

"Then whoever it was must have shot this arrow from a distance. Yet the aim was almost perfect." He leaned forward and put his elbows on the table. "Denis, we must think. Part of this, of course, is my fault. I didn't realize the danger would be so great in Wyndhamshire. If the baron is behind the war, I assumed that since he was back home we would be safe. But apparently his henchmen have followed us. I only hope they haven't tracked us here."

"We were careful," I assured him. "Even tonight, as we brought Alinor home."

"Good. Max is already in the barn repairing the carriage. We should probably leave within the next day or so. If the king of Wyndhamshire has already ordered the river rerouted, things look really bad."

He stood up. "Let's get some sleep. First thing tomorrow I'm going back to the palace to meet the king. You remember the doctor said he wanted to see me alone. I want you and Jane and Max to walk over to that grocery shop two or three blocks down the street and order supplies for the trip home. We'll pick them up with the wagon on the way out of town. Go by the back pastures, as usual."

16

The next morning as we ate one of Mrs. Bock's excellent breakfasts Sir Robert again warned us to be careful. Then he thanked his hostess for the meal, mounted his horse, and wended his way through the pasture to the far gate.

"Let's go get the supplies," I said to my friends as I got up from the table.

Max groaned. "Do we *all* have to go? Now that I've got new underbraces I need to keep working on that carriage."

As we walked to the door I winked at him. "I presume we'll be getting the genuine Judde quality workmanship."

He glared at me. "Of course."

"I can't pay you 150 shillings for your work, but please remember to carve your coat of arms into it."

"Denis," he said dangerously, "I'm warning you—"

"What are you guys talking about?" asked a mystified Jane.

"Nothing," I chuckled, then sobered up. Max can take just so much ribbing and that's it. "We'd better all go to the store. Sir Robert wants us to stick together."

"Alinor too?" Max sounded doubtful.

"I'm OK," Alinor said quickly.

"Are you sure?" I asked. "Jane, what do you think?"

Jane frowned thoughtfully at Alinor. "Did that green tea help?"

Alinor made a face. "What was that, anyway? It was almost worse than getting shot by a crossbow."

"Good," Jane nodded with satisfaction. "That shows it got where it needed to go. Well," she said, "you can try to come along if you want."

"I'm fine, really."

"And *I'm* not supposed to let you out of my sight," I told her. She made another face at me. "I can take care of myself."

"Yeah, just like yesterday," Max said.

"Hey," I said, "knock it off. Let's get going."

We said goodbye to Mrs. Bock. Even though the store was only about three blocks away, we left the house one by one, at intervals of several minutes, heading across the pastures in the opposite direction so as not to arouse suspicion. As we skirted the pastures in order to approach Ashton from the north, I noticed again the high stone tower looming over the town.

"Look," I said, pointing. "There's somebody up there. At the top, behind the railing."

"A man," Alinor said.

"A woman," Jane corrected confidently. She had the best vision of any of us. "A woman with white hair."

"Are you sure?" Max asked. "You can't see that far."

"Sure I'm sure."

We reached the little grocery shop in a few moments. The shopkeeper turned out to be chatty and also very curious.

"You sure you're going to need all these supplies?" he asked.

"Where are you going?"

"Oh, out of town," I said.

"You kids traveling by yourselves?"

"No."

"Who's going with you?"

"A friend of ours."

He filled our order, and then said, "Hey, how you kids going to carry all this?"

"We'll pick it up later."

"Want me to deliver it?"

"No, that's all right."

"I'd be glad to deliver it. Where are you staying?"

"No, we'll be OK," I insisted. "We'll stop by to pick it up tomorrow or the next day."

"Suit yourself," he said, shrugging his shoulders. He glanced at Max. "Hey, buddy," he said, "you're not going to eat all those dried apples right now, are you?"

Max grinned. "Sorry. I like them."

"You eat too many of 'em and you'll be screaming for Doctor Skotia."

"Who's he?" Max asked casually.

"*She*, you mean," said the shopkeeper. "A woman doctor."

Jane glanced at me. "Do they really have a woman doctor in this country?" she asked the shopkeeper.

"Sure do," he replied. "She's the palace physician."

"So if Max needed her," I said, "he'd have to go to the palace."

"Nope." He shook his head. "She lives here in this town."

He grinned and tapped his forehead. "Some folks think she's a little off in the head. Probably because of all that doctor study she's done."

The trio of young people became very attentive to his words.

"She lives here?" Max asked.

"Yep. Right up there in that big tower, a couple blocks over. Look, pull that door open a little."

Jane obediently tugged on it, and it swung inward.

"You can see it out there, through the doorway to the left. Dr. Skotia owns that tower. She's lived there for a long time. Must be 10, 15 years now."

Alinor crossed the floor and stepped out. Shading her eyes, she glanced upward to the left. "There's someone standing up there," she reported.

"That'd be the doctor," said the shopkeeper.

Jane peered around the door frame and looked for herself.

"It's a man," she said.

"You said it was a woman before," Max said in a low voice.

"It's a man."

"Can't be," chuckled the shopkeeper.

"Why not?" I asked.

"No chance of that," he said. "She lives there by herself, and she never lets anyone else in. Ain't no men in *her* life!"

Jane stepped away from the door, and Alinor also turned to re-enter the shop.

Suddenly there was a tremendous *whack*. A thick-shafted arrow jutted from the door, right where Alinor had been standing.

Whirling, she stared at the arrow, screamed, and went white.

Max leaped for the door and slammed it shut.

"Max!" I shouted. "Get the arrow!"

Swiftly he pulled open the door again, crouching out of range, and twisted and yanked at the shaft. Finally it jerked free, and he slammed the door and shot the bolt.

"What happened?" barked the shopkeeper. "What's going on here?"

Jane helped Alinor to her feet. "Are you OK?"

Alinor nodded weakly. "Let's get out of here."

"What happened?" snapped the shopkeeper. "You kids playing some game on me?"

Without speaking, Max held up the arrow, an ugly one. "It's from the same fletcher as yesterday's."

Now it was the shopkeeper's turn to grow faint. He clutched the counter. "Get out!" he choked. "Get out of my shop."

We stared at him.

"Get out!" He reached behind him for a large knife, hefted it, and came around the counter. "Leave! Right now!"

"Sir," I said quickly. "You don't understand. Someone out there just shot a crossbow arrow at this girl."

"Get out," he repeated, stepping closer to us. He motioned toward the door.

Jane's eyes blazed. "We'll die if we walk through that door!"

"I don't know who you people are, and I don't want to," howled the shopkeeper. "And I don't want anything to do with you. I'm a law-abiding man, and I don't want to be mixed up with people who get shot at. Out. Quick, or I swear I'll—"

I spoke quickly. "Do you have a back door, sir? We may be able to escape if we could—"

"That way," he gasped, pointing. "Back there. Hurry! I will count to five. One . . . two . . . three—"

We hurried toward the back of the shop, struggled with a heavy latch, and burst out onto a covered porch.

CHAPTER
17

We flattened ourselves against the outside wall.

"That stupid coward," Max growled.

"Shhhh!" hissed Jane.

My mind was working quickly. "Max! Did you notice the angle of that arrow as it stuck in the door?"

He paused. "It looked like it slanted downward. Why?"

"It was shot from a height."

"The tower!" he breathed.

"There was a man up there," Jane said emphatically. "I saw him."

"You've got the sharpest eyes of any of us," I said to her. "What did he look like?"

Jane thought a moment, then shook her head. "No. I can't say for sure, exactly. He was just a dark blob against the sky."

Max asked, "Was he tall? Short?"

"I don't know."

"Let's go," said Alinor faintly. Her face was very white.

Jane turned to her, concerned. Then she said to Max and me, "She's weak. We'd better get her home."

"Fine," I agreed, "and what'll happen if we walk away from here? Whoever's in that tower knows where we are, and you can bet he's got that crossbow cocked and ready."

"Maybe they're coming down after us," whispered Alinor.

Max shook his head. "I doubt it."

"Right," I said. "This isn't a big city like Wyndhamshire where everybody minds their own business and you can get away with just about anything. This is a sleepy little village, and anybody who showed himself and tried to start something would soon have a lot of nosy onlookers. He took a risk in even firing the crossbow."

"But we can't stay here forever," Alinor said.

At this point a terrific clanging broke out. It sounded like someone was beating on a bell with great force.

"What's that?" Alinor asked, terrified.

"Fire bell." Max grinned with satisfaction.

"Yeah," I said. "The worst thing that could happen in a village, but the best thing that could happen to *us*."

The clanging was deafening, but above it we could now hear the shouts of villagers as they poured into the streets, carrying heavy wooden buckets filled with water.

"Bucket brigade," said Max.

"How's this going to help us?" Jane asked.

"Simple," I said. "Let's just start walking and mingle with the crowd. The guy in the tower won't dare try anything. I'll bet when he heard the bell he ducked back inside. Let's go."

I'll admit that my own legs were trembling a little as we strode across the meadow behind the store. When we could see the tower again Max glanced up at it. "Ha!" he chuckled. "Not a sign of him."

"Alinor, you OK?" Jane gripped Alinor's arm tightly.

"Let go of me." Alinor jerked away. "I don't want to attract any attention and have people asking questions."

Villagers, armed with buckets, continued to rush by us.

"Might as well just follow the crowd," said Max. "Looks like everybody's going our way."

As we turned a corner we saw why. And I was sorry we'd been glad about the fire bell.

"The Bock house!" I gasped.

The heavy thatched roof of the cottage was burning a brilliant orange. Thick black clouds of smoke boiled up into the sky.

Jane suddenly cried out, "Mrs. Bock! What about her?"

We broke into a run, even Alinor.

"You stay here," Jane urged her.

"No," Alinor insisted firmly. "Just hold onto my hand." Together, the girls ran behind us.

Max and I rounded the barn first and reached the farmyard. Villagers had formed a long line from a nearby pond and were passing buckets from hand to hand and throwing silvery ropes of water high up on to the roof.

"Looks like they're getting it," Max breathed thankfully.

Jane hurried up to join us.

"Where's Alinor?" I asked.

"I hid her in the barn, under some hay," Jane said. "She didn't like it, but I thought it was safer. Have you seen Mrs. Bock yet?"

"I think she's over there where all those women are clustering around," Max said. "Can you get close enough to check her out?"

"I'll try." Jane darted over to the circle of women. "I'm staying with Mrs. Bock," we heard her say. "Let me through. I'm staying with her. I know what to do."

The women drew back, and I could now see Mrs. Bock lying flat on her back. Jane began massaging her arms and hands.

Suddenly, from behind us, came glad cries. "The doctor! Make way for Dr. Skotia!"

"Don't show her your face," I said to Max in a low

voice. "Let's duck down and pretend we're playing marbles or something."

From a crouching position I watched the tall, white-haired doctor stride along, carrying her canvas bag. She knelt down beside Mrs. Bock, where Jane was still massaging her arms.

"Good, good." Dr. Skotia's deep, cracked voice carried clearly into our ears. "That's right. Who are you, child?"

"My name is Jane. I'm staying here. With Mrs. Bock."

The doctor looked at her closely. "How long have you been here? Are you her grandchild?"

Jane kept massaging Mrs. Bock's arms. "Please, doctor. Can't you help her?"

"You're doing fine yourself," said Dr. Skotia. "You certainly know how to treat a case of fainting." She bent over Mrs. Bock, lifted one of her eyelids and let it close again, and took her pulse. "Shock," she said. "She'll be all right." She untied her bag, rummaged in it, and brought forth a bottle. "Now listen carefully," she instructed Jane. "Three times a day I want you to make your grandmother a glass of warm milk. Into that milk I want you to put three pinches of this powder. Stir it well, and then give it to her."

Jane nodded.

"You will do that, without fail?"

Jane nodded again.

"I will come in three days to see her," said Dr. Skotia. She arose, towering over the rest of the women, and stalked away.

After she'd gone, Jane stood up too. "Please, can some of you help me?" she asked, looking around at the women. "Can we carry Mrs. Bock into the barn there?"

The carriage had been stored in the barn, and Max and I followed as the women transported the moaning Mrs. Bock directly to the lowest of the two bunk-hammocks inside. Alinor was nowhere in sight.

"I can take care of her now," Jane told the women. "Thank you for helping."

Shortly after the women had gone, Mrs. Bock awoke. After blinking a few times and inquiring where on earth she was, she announced that she was feeling fine. "Don't mind about me now, children," she murmured weakly. "I'll be up and about in a bit."

"No, you won't," Jane said earnestly. "You stay where you are until I say you can get up."

Alinor emerged from behind a pile of hay. "Denis, has Sir Robert come back yet?"

"Not yet."

"Well, it doesn't really matter."

I looked at her curiously. "What doesn't matter?"

She didn't answer, but turned away.

The day wore on. We all instinctively knew that keeping busy would help pass the time. So Jane hovered over Mrs. Bock, and Max divided his time between carriage repair and making notes on any fixing the house would need. I glanced over at him once in a while, and I could tell by the careful way he worked that he didn't seem to be allowing the apprentice's ideas to affect him.

I found a flat board for a writing desk, opened my journal, and began to write an account of the day's happenings. How long I wrote I don't know—I was concentrating so hard that everything else was oblivious to me.

But suddenly Jane stood beside me. "Where's Alinor?" she asked.

I looked up. "I don't know. Is she over at the house?"

"No. Once Max checked everything out, he boarded it up so looters couldn't get in. He's been helping me look for her. We can't find her anywhere."

18

A ball of ice formed just below my heart. "You checked everywhere?"

"Everywhere."

My voice rose. "You're sure?"

"Shhh." Jane glanced behind her. "Mrs. Bock is sleeping again. I don't want her to know. Yes, I looked all around."

Max came running through the door. "The neighbors haven't seen her," he panted.

"Is Angel gone too?"

"Yeah," he said.

There was a squeezing sensation in my chest. "Let's go outside where we can talk."

"Jane," I said once we were in the barnyard, "did Alinor give any hint of where she might have gone?"

Jane thought a moment. "Yeah. Remember when we came into the pasture and saw the house burning? You guys ran on ahead, right?"

"Go on."

"And Alinor kept babbling about the king."

"Which king?"

"I'm not sure. She kept saying things like, 'If only I could get to the palace.' "

I took Jane by the shoulders. "Listen to me carefully."

"Ouch! You're hurting me."

"Think back. This is important. Try to remember exactly what she said. Was it 'palace' or was it 'castle'?"

"Palace."

"Are you sure?"

"Let go," she demanded. "Sure, I'm sure!"

I released her and ran inside the barn to where my stallion was munching on a wisp of hay.

"Denis," Max called out, "what're you doing?"

I saddled the horse quickly. "Alinor's headed for Wyndhamshire. I'm going to try to find her."

"You'd better wait for Sir Robert."

"Max, I'll run you down if you don't get out of the way."

He stepped aside, and I thundered through the open door and out onto the main road. It was late afternoon by now, and the sun was just touching the treetops in the west.

As I galloped, fear and self-loathing grew inside me. *I've failed the king again,* I thought to myself in agony. *Am I worth anything at all? Is my whole character flawed? I'm so unfaithful. He really can't depend on me after all.*

You couldn't help it that she ran off, a little voice in my head reasoned.

Yes, I could have, I disagreed. *Alinor's not thinking right. She's in anguish because being in Wyndhamshire brings back memories. She went to the cemetery and never got to see her parents' resting place. She's been shot at twice by a crossbow. And she has the further pressure of wondering whether her presence at Mrs. Bock's house was the cause of the fire.*

But you really can't be blamed, the voice insisted.

Yes I can. She's worried about the war between two great, friendly countries. She's scared that everything her grandfather worked for will disappear in less than two weeks. You can't expect anyone to think straight under pressure like that. And it was my duty to watch over her when she couldn't watch over herself.

The little voice had no more to say. Because there wasn't any more to say.

"If anything has happened to Alinor," I said aloud, "I'm never going back to my country. I'd never be able to face my king."

But he loves you. The little voice broke its silence again.

"He won't love me if I killed his granddaughter," I answered bleakly.

Don't be silly.

"I killed her," I repeated.

But he loves you.

And this time it was I who was quiet.

* * * *

I don't know what I thought I was going to accomplish by dashing off toward Wyndhamshire that way. All along the route I watched for Alinor and Angel, but saw nothing. I even took the risk of asking a couple farmers if they'd seen a girl ride by on a horse. They said they'd just come from across the pasture and weren't sure.

I made it to the palace in what was probably record time, and first went around to the cemetery. After tying my horse to an iron fence bar, I squeezed through the same opening we'd used before and wandered up and down among the gravestones. She wasn't there. The open grave had been closed in.

I went to the palace gate, found the page boy on duty, and asked him if a girl had come there. He said no.

So there was nothing to do but to ride through a few of the main streets on the off chance I might see Angel, and then travel back to the Bock farm.

It was dark when I guided the horse into the Bock

driveway. There was a movement in the darkness, and Max approached.

"It's about time," he said. "What did you learn?"

I slid off the stallion and gripped its halter. "Nothing."

"Sir Robert's not back either."

I drew in a sharp breath. "He's not?"

"No. No message. Nothing."

"Everybody else safe in the barn?"

"Yeah," Max said. "I waited out here to meet you so we could talk without worrying them. Denis, what are we going to do?"

"You tell me and we'll both know."

"I get this feeling that things are falling apart," he said darkly. "You'd think that Sir Robert could take care of himself all right."

"Speaking of falling apart, you'd better get that carriage fixed. We might have to get out of here on a moment's notice."

"I fixed it. This afternoon."

I eyed him meaningfully. "Listen, buddy, I hope you didn't use some sort of gimcrack system."

He gave me a level gaze. "Don't worry about that carriage. I completely replaced the underbrace. The four spares I bought the other day in Wyndhamshire are top quality. Any other questions?" There was a challenge in his voice.

"No, no," I said hastily.

"Did you really think I bought into that baloney those apprentices were feeding me?"

"You seemed pretty enchanted by it."

"Well, maybe for a little. It was all that cash that dazzled my eyes. But that's all behind me."

"Good."

"And don't ever get it into your head again that I'd endanger our lives with a quick-fix repair job. OK?"

"All right, all *right*."

Suddenly a voice spoke behind me out of the darkness. "Denis?"

"Jane," I gurgled. "You scared me."

"Did you find Alinor?"

"No."

She was silent. "I guess I never expected it. Come in the barn. I want to show you something."

Max and I followed her. I penned the stallion, and Jane got a lighted candle from the carriage and led us to a far corner of the barn.

"Look."

"Where?"

"There, by that box."

"What is it?" Max asked.

"A rat. It's dead."

I sighed wearily. "OK, you have my deepest sympathy. What do you want me to do, conduct a funeral service?"

Fear lurked in her voice. "It was that powder."

My jaw went slack.

"That powder for Mrs. Bock," she continued. "I got suspicious about it, so I put some on a piece of cheese and set it here. And just now I heard a rat squeaking. I came over and found it, dead."

19

I turned to face Jane. "Did you give Mrs. Bock any of the powder?"

"Of course not."

Mrs. Bock's voice called from the carriage. "Children? Are you there?"

"Yes, we're here," Max answered.

"Sounds like she's healthy." I wiped sweat off my forehead. "Where's the bottle?"

"I hid it," Jane said.

"Good," I approved. "Now, listen. The three of us have got to sit down and do some serious plotting."

"Let's get to bed," Jane said.

I looked at her in annoyance. "I can't sleep knowing that Alinor is out there somewhere, probably in the clutches of the doctor. Or whoever shot that crossbow."

"We need our rest," Jane insisted.

"If you can sleep, fine!" I snapped. "You too, Max."

Max raised his arms above his head and yawned. "She's right, Denis. I can't think straight when I'm tired, and neither can you. Back home I've seen you cook up some pretty weird ideas late at night."

"Come on, Denis," Jane pleaded.

"Well, where do I sleep?" I growled. "You and Mrs. Bock have got the bunks."

"Let's sack out on that haystack over there by the window," Max suggested.

I glared in the direction he pointed. An open window framed a picture of bright stars and a section of moon. Without a word, I stalked over to the pile of hay and flung myself down. I stared up into the full face of the moon.

About 10 minutes later I heard a rustling, then a footstep on the floor. "Denis?" It was Jane's voice. "Drink this."

I heaved myself up. Into the shaft of moonlight came a slender hand bearing a steaming mug.

"It's herb tea," she said. "My own recipe."

I took the mug and sniffed. "How'd you get it hot?"

"That little blacksmith forge in the next room. I keep a bed of coals going there. That's how we cooked supper while you were gone."

I sipped the tea until the cup was empty. "Thanks," I said gratefully. "Sorry I've been rude. I guess I'm so worried about Alinor that—" Suddenly I couldn't speak any more.

"Yeah," she said softly. "I kind of like her myself."

* * * *

I had a strange dream that night. It seemed as though the moon was bright, intensely bright, and that outside the open window I heard a strange, hoarse, whispery voice speaking. Then my king's voice replied, and it seemed that once he floated before the window, wearing a striped robe. And then a thunderous pounding began, a jarring and jolting *bang-bang-bang* that seemed to rock the world on its foundations.

I rolled over and sat up. The moon had vanished, and the morning sun blazed through the window. The banging was now loud and real, and I discovered that somebody was kicking or beating on the barn door.

"Who's that?" called Max from another pile of hay.

"I'll find out," I said. "I didn't know you'd locked the doors."

"I figured it was safest."

I hurried to the door and peered out through a crack. Then I gave an amazed yell of delight, yanked the crossbar away, and swung the door inward.

"Who is it?" called Mrs. Bock from the door of the carriage.

"It's Squire Forster!" I shouted.

"Hello, there, young Denis," said Squire Forster as he hobbled through the doorway, supporting himself on a makeshift crutch. He was a thin man with a salt-and-pepper goatee, and he leaned heavily on a makeshift cane. "Thought I'd never get you people up in here."

Max and a very drowsy Jane, wearing puzzled looks, had joined us now.

"This is Squire Forster," I said to the others. "He was the castle scribe until he retired recently. I took over his job. He's got family living in Wyndhamshire, and he came over here to be with them." I stared at him curiously. "But how did you know we were in here?"

"Well, I couldn't rouse anybody at the house, and when I looked up at the roof I saw why. I happened to glance over here at the barn and saw a little wisp of smoke coming out of the blacksmith chimney, and I figured this was where you were staying after the fire. Is Emmelina all right?"

"Mrs. Bock? Sure, she's in the carriage." Jane pointed.

"Good. I wonder if I could find a place to sit down." He grimaced in pain.

"What happened to you?" I asked.

"Here," Jane said quickly. She dragged over a large bucket and overturned it. "Are you hurt?"

"Yes," he said, sinking gratefully onto the seat. "Fell

off my horse late last week. Not sure if I broke my leg, or what."

"Let me check." Jane knelt quickly beside him, running her fingers deftly over his leg.

"Ouch! There."

Jane poked and prodded a moment, and the old squire grunted in pain. "If it's broken, it's not a clean break," she decided finally. "I could make you a splint to keep it steady."

He smiled through his pain. "You should work for Dr. Skotia." He looked around again. "Where's Emmelina? Are you sure she's safe?"

"Of course, I'm safe." Mrs. Bock approached us. "How are you, Forster?"

"Forgive me for not standing, Emmelina," he said, "but it looks like I broke my leg."

"Oh, no," she said, alarmed. "How did it happen?"

Squire Forster paused and looked around at us. "I think the best thing would be for me to start at the beginning," he said. "Where is Sir Robert?"

"He's gone to Wyndhamshire, I think," I said.

He paused again. "Then let me tell you a story. It may explain several things. I was good friends with Bock, Prince Geoffrey's squire. Bock, as you know, was very devoted to Prince Geoffrey, and approved of all he was doing to spread our king's ideas of freedom and democracy. And those ideas were becoming popular here."

"Right," I nodded. "The Wyndhamshire king abandoned his castle and began to live in town."

Squire Forster glanced at me. "How much have you heard? Have you heard of the duel?"

I filled him in on what we knew.

"Good," he said. "You know more than I thought. But that's not the whole story, by any means. You'll remember they met in the palace garden, and both young men were killed."

"Yes," said Mrs. Bock, "and the evidence seems clear that for some reason Prince Geoffrey murdered Prince Andrew. My own husband admitted this on his deathbed."

Squire Forster nodded. "That's what he told you. And he believed it when he told it to you. But Emmelina, remember that I saw him alone a few days after he told his story to the doctor."

She stared at him. "That's right. You did."

"Yes. And what he told me was entirely different, something that explains the whole mystery."

20

Let me tell you how Bock finally discovered the truth," said Squire Forster. "You remember, Denis, that after I had initiated you to your new duties, my wife and I came here."

I nodded. "To live with your relatives."

"Right. Well, shortly after I arrived I visited the Bocks and discovered to my sorrow that he was very ill. Dr. Skotia was in the room with him when I came in. When Bock saw me, his eyes lit up. We greeted each other and talked over the old times a little.

"Then he paused and glanced at Dr. Skotia, then back to me, and said, 'I must tell you both something very important.' And then he told us the story you already know—how he was waiting in the darkness holding the two princes' swords, how suddenly he heard Prince Geoffrey's voice asking for his sword, and how after hearing loud cries he rushed into the garden and found both men dead, Geoffrey clutching his own sword, and Andrew a small dagger."

Squire Forster paused.

Jane shivered.

"And as you know," he continued, "Dr. Skotia went right to the palace and told the king everything. And that's when the hostilities began between the two countries.

"Over the next few days my friend grew rapidly worse.

Late one night I was again summoned to his bedside."

Emmelina Bock nodded. "He begged me to send for you."

"Yes, and you remember that he asked you to leave the bedroom and close the door. When you were gone, he fixed his eyes on me. They were wide with terror—partly from delirium, and partly from the knowledge of a horrible truth that had just dawned upon him.

"Dr. Skotia had been to see him a short time earlier that evening. After giving him his medicine, she stepped out of his bedroom and spent some time chatting with you, Emmelina, in the kitchen."

"I remember," said Mrs. Bock sadly. "She was telling me a story about Prince Geoffrey, something humorous he had once said."

"Exactly," said Squire Forster. "Bock lay on his bed, half-listening to the conversation, and suddenly he heard the sound of Prince Geoffrey's voice! For a moment he thought he was going mad, and he nearly called out in terror. But he kept quiet.

"As the two of you continued to speak, he knew: *It was Dr. Skotia herself, imitating the Prince's accents perfectly!*

"And then, with a rush, it all came home to him. Trembling with rage and terror, he could hardly wait for Dr. Skotia to go. You remember, Emmelina, that he sent for me immediately."

She nodded. "I truly thought he had lost his mind," she quavered. "His eyes burned from his poor fevered face. He begged me to send you to him quickly."

"When I arrived," the squire continued, "he gasped out his suspicion into my ears: Dr. Skotia had been behind the murder. It was she, and not Prince Geoffrey, who stood close to him in that dark garden and asked for the sword. Then she, or some assistant—although she herself is a terribly strong woman—had suddenly rushed upon the two princes.

"Since she is a doctor she would know exactly where to strike, and you may be sure she struck accurately. She then placed the sword in Geoffrey's hand, then drew Andrew's dagger and placed it in his."

Squire Forster paused. "And no sooner had Bock gasped this information into my ears than he fell into a coma from which I sensed he would never awaken."

Mrs. Bock was now weeping. "Oh, the poor, dear man," she sobbed. "He died with that horrible truth on his mind."

"But his face was at peace," said the squire softly. "He had done his duty. I, of course, recognized that this information must be revealed at once. But how was I to do this? I knew that no one would believe me at the Wyndhamshire palace because I was not known there—and Dr. Skotia would be sure to testify against me. Yet someone in power should know.

"Suddenly I decided to return to my country and tell His Majesty, Geoffrey's father. Perhaps he would be able to do something through diplomatic channels. So I went back home, tiptoed into my house, and took three loaves of bread from the breadbox for nourishment along the way. I didn't even waken my wife—I seized a charcoal from the fireplace and scrawled her a note on the wall. I knew she would find someone to read it for her.

"I got on my horse and headed for my country. I rode almost nonstop, scarcely halting to sleep. One night I rode through a terrible thunderstorm. That's when I fell off the horse. Later, I almost stopped to rest under a wagon that was parked beside the road, but I kept riding onward."

"That was our wagon!" I exclaimed.

"This one?" He stared over my shoulder at the long-wagon.

"I saw you that night," I said. "I was awake. It's too bad you didn't stop."

"Yes, it would have saved everyone a lot of trouble. Well, anyway," he continued, "I arrived at the king's castle late the next day and informed him of everything. He told me that Sir Robert and the rest of you were on your way here, so after I had rested myself and my horse, I immediately started back to find you and help take care of you."

He looked around. "That reminds me. Where's the princess? Is she still asleep?"

There were a few seconds of silence. "She's gone," I said.

"Gone! Where?"

"We don't know," Jane said. "She just left. Yesterday afternoon sometime. Her horse is gone, too."

"Did she give any hint, any—"

"Nothing," I said.

"Do you know where Dr. Skotia lives?" he asked quickly.

"Sure," Jane said. "The tower."

"Which tower?"

"Surely you've seen it, Squire Forster," Mrs. Bock said. "The tall one here in Ashton. Dr. Skotia owns those buildings."

"Ah," said the squire with satisfaction. "A great light has broken upon me. Now I understand everything."

"What do you mean?" asked Max.

Squire Forster gazed at us thoughtfully. "No," he finally said, "if something goes wrong and they capture you, you can say you knew nothing."

"But what about Alinor?" worried Jane.

"I must go to Wyndhamshire," said the squire.

I threw out my hands in a dissatisfied gesture. "But when are you coming back?"

"As soon as I have accomplished my purpose."

"Please, Squire Forster," begged Jane. "Let us help you."

"It is no place for children."

My chin went up. "I'm a squire, too, sir. If there is danger, I demand to have my part in it."

His eyes leveled with mine. "You may be a squire, but you are a boy. There are many things you do not understand."

My mouth went dry with rage, but I kept my voice respectful.

"Please, Squire Forster."

"Stay right here," he commanded.

"By whose authority, sir?"

His eyebrows rose. "By my gray hairs."

I said nothing.

He reached for his cane and hobbled to his feet. "I will return as soon as I can."

"But your leg could be broken," cried Jane.

"Forster," pleaded Mrs. Bock, "you can't travel like that."

"Peace, Emmelina. All will be over soon." He limped out the door, closing it firmly behind him. We heard the whinny of a horse, then the clattering of hooves.

21

We stood in silence. Then I slammed my fist against the closed door. It shuddered open to reveal an empty driveway. A glossy ball of blood began to grow on my skinned knuckle.

"You'll get gangrene," Jane said automatically.

"Who cares?" I snarled.

"*You'd* care if you lost your arm," she said peevishly.

"Well, where does he get off anyway?" I howled. "First he's so informative, and then all of a sudden he clams up."

Mrs. Bock tried to soothe me. "Oh, that's just the way he is."

Max stared down the empty road. "Shall we follow him?"

"Don't be silly, Max," I said bitterly. "We're supposed to stay here in our baby's playpen, cozy and warm, when who knows what could be happening to Alinor? She and Sir Robert may be in that tower."

"If they're in the tower there's nothing we can do about it," Max said grimly. "It's a miniature castle. The lowest windows are at least 50 feet above ground. There's only one huge door at the base, and I'll bet it's locked."

"It *is* locked," Mrs. Bock said.

We turned to her curiously.

"How do you know?" Max asked.

Mrs. Bock smiled. "I cooked for the doctor for several years before I retired."

I stared at her. "Then you know the tower well?"

"Very well."

"Mrs. Bock," I said carefully, "please tell us all you know about the tower."

Of course, once Emmelina Bock discovered that we were serious about going to the tower, she clammed up. It took Max and Jane and me until about 11:00 that night before she finally weakened.

"I really can't let you children go," she said, her voice trembling. "What could you do?"

"Maybe nothing," I said. "Maybe we'd just be a scouting party. If Alinor's grandfather sends over a strike force, it would help them if they knew for sure she was in the tower."

"It's almost midnight," Max said. "This'd be the best time."

Finally she sighed. "All right, then. Listen very carefully."

An hour later, Max, Jane, and I were crouching in the moonlight in the high grass on the edge of the doctor's estate. Max's hands cupped a thick piece of leather that formed a sort of nest for a small metal box. Jane clutched a cloth bag containing pieces of raw meat sprinkled generously with Dr. Skotia's powder, in case the doctor kept watchdogs.

Thirty feet away from us, across a smooth lawn, a tiny shed gleamed whitely in the light of the moon.

"Here comes a cloud," whispered Jane.

I leaned forward tensely. "Let's go for it. Ready? *Now!*"

The cloud passed before the moon, and the lawn dimmed. We scrambled across the bare grass, reaching the black shadow of the shed just as the white brilliance reappeared.

I reached into my backpack and withdrew a rusted ring of giant keys. "Good thing Mrs. Bock still had these," I muttered. "Too bad the doctor didn't trust her with the key to the main door."

One by one I fitted the huge keys into a keyhole. The third one turned gratingly.

"Quiet," breathed Jane.

"Max, help me push."

We braced our shoulders against the door, and with a heart-chilling *squawk* it swung inward. We stepped quickly inside.

Jane stood still, moving only her eyes. "It's dark in here."

"Good."

I dug in my backpack and found a huge tallow candle Mrs. Bock had given us.

Max fumbled gingerly with the box he carried. The lid popped off to reveal a few glowing coals from the blacksmith's furnace. Max blew these into life, and I touched the candle's wick to them.

"Yuck!" Jane exclaimed as the candle flared, revealing a clutter of old wheelbarrows and rags.

"The trap door should be right about—here." Max kicked aside a rotted blanket to reveal a square wooden door, hinged on one edge, set into the floor. "Give me a hand, Denis."

I handed the candle to Jane, and Max and I tugged on the ring in the center of the door. Finally the door swung up.

"There's the tunnel, just like she told us," I exulted, peering down into the darkness. "But it looks like there's standing water down there." I grabbed a long stick and prodded the floor of the tunnel. "Not too deep. About an

inch. She said the floor slopes upward, so it'll be drier further on. Ready?"

I jumped down into the darkness, my feet smacking into the water. Max followed. Jane peered down, a thoughtful look on her face.

"Jane," Max said. "You OK?"

"Yeah," she said finally. "Hold this." She handed the candle down and joined us.

The tunnel obviously hadn't been used for several years. Shiny-backed lizards scuttled ahead of us, and huge spiders rustled slightly in their webs.

"Toss that poisoned meat behind us," I instructed Jane. "If there are rats, that'll keep them busy." She flung the meat away from her, and we could hear it *splat* in the water.

"I didn't think the tunnel would be this small," I grunted. "It can't be any more than five feet high." I hunched down and began walking slowly. Jane fell into step behind me, and Max brought up the rear.

"Careful with that candle," he cautioned. "I'm not sure how much spark's left in my coals."

The tunnel actually grew smaller and narrower the farther we went. I felt smothered and closed in, almost like the top and sides were squeezing me. I wanted to straighten up, to press my shoulders in panic against the ceiling.

"How much longer?" Jane panted.

For what seemed like an eternity we scrunched along. Ahead of us was nothing but darkness. My back ached. I almost turned back, but the thought that Alinor might be in that tower urged me forward.

"Where's the end of this rat hole?" Max's voice echoed hollowly.

"Look." I pointed.

Up ahead we could see a large iron-strapped door. The

sight cheered us, and as we hurried forward the tunnel grew larger, so that by the time we got to the door we were standing upright.

"You OK, Jane?" I asked.

"Sure," she said, her eyes large with relief. Then she glanced at my hand. "Denis," she said firmly, "you're not going a step further until I look at your knuckle."

"Forget about my knuckle. It's OK."

"No, it's not. Look, it's bleeding again."

"Who cares?"

"You'll get—"

"Jane, you're paranoid. This is just a little cut."

"Let me bandage it."

Max sighed. "Better let Doctor Jane do her duty."

"You guys think I'm crazy, but I'm not." Jane fumbled in her pocket and pulled out a piece of cloth. As she began to tear it, the candle gleamed down upon its pattern.

My breath forsook me. "Jane," I whispered, "where did you get that?"

22

Jane quickly bandaged my hand, then glanced up at me curiously. "Where did I get what?"

"That cloth? I recognize it from somewhere."

She frowned at it. "I found it outside this morning. But it's clean."

"Outside where?"

"Denis," Max snorted, "we're wasting time. Quit babbling about that cloth. We can talk about it later."

"*Where*, Jane?"

She looked at me thoughtfully. "Out by the window."

"That window I was sleeping beside?"

"I guess so."

I took a deep breath. My head was whirling. "Thanks. That's all I needed to know. Jane, hold this candle." I fished in my backpack for the key ring. Once by one, I thrust the rusty keys into the keyhole, and carefully turned them.

"None of them work," I reported. "I always come up against this hard piece of metal."

"Maybe Mrs. Bock lost the key to this door," Jane suggested.

"No, she told us she had them all, except the outside tower door, of course." I stared thoughtfully through the keyhole.

Max said, "Let me try the keys."

"It's no use," I said.

"Give me them."

"I told you, I tried them."

"Come on," he urged. "Let me try."

He took the ring and inserted the keys one by one. When he'd tried two or three, he stopped and exploded into muffled laughter.

"Quiet!" hissed Jane.

"Denis, you dummy. The reason we haven't been able to work the keys is that it's not locked."

"You're kidding."

"No, I'm not kidding. I've installed enough locks on chests and cupboards to know what the key feels like when you can't turn it any further. All we have to do is open the door."

"Be careful," Jane breathed.

"It's dark through the keyhole," said Max. "But you're right—I'll try it alone first." He set the ring of keys carefully on the floor, grasped the metal handle tightly, put his shoulder against the door, and pushed.

"I told you it was locked," I agreed.

"It's not locked, it's stuck," he replied. "Help me."

Together we shouldered the door. No movement at all.

"We can't kick it, I suppose."

Max thought for a moment. "Better not. Wait. I've got it." He picked up the key ring. "Which is the key to the shed?"

"That one."

"You sure?"

"Yeah. I remember that scratch on the side of the shank."

"Great," he said. "If it breaks, no big deal. We don't need it anymore."

"But that doesn't fit this door," I objected. "What's your plan?"

"Watch me." He stared thoughtfully at the key. It was huge, probably eight inches long. With his right index finger he felt along the crack between the door and the stone flooring. When he found a wide space, he slid one end of the key under it. "Now, let's hope this works," he murmured.

Grasping the key's handle, he levered it cautiously upward. The door didn't move. He thrust the key still further underneath and heaved again. There was a sharp *crack* that sent my heart leaping into my throat.

Max glued his eye to the keyhole. Jane and I waited impatiently.

"See anything?" I asked.

"Not yet," he replied. "Still dark. I think I loosened the door in its frame. Let's go!"

"Wait a few more minutes," I said. "Just in case."

As we sat there in the candle glow, Jane asked, "What will we do if we get up to the tower?"

I shrugged. "Who knows? I suppose we just play it by ear."

"I wonder if she's OK," Jane said.

"I do too," I replied. "Let's hope so."

Max peered through the keyhole again. "I think we're safe."

He and I stood to our feet and braced our shoulders against the door. This time, as our shoulders moved forward, the door moved too, creaking loudly.

"Just inch it along," I directed through clenched teeth.

After a few seconds of work the gap was wide enough for us to slip through sideways, one by one. Jane came last, with the candle.

The room in which we were standing must have been some kind of kitchen at one time. Great meat hooks projected from the walls, and cobwebby shelves sagged under heavy, lidded jars. Beside one of the shelves on the opposite side of the room stood a door.

"Now from what Mrs. Bock says, that big door must lead to the room where the staircase is," I mused.

Max held up his hand. "Wait a minute. Didn't she say that the lower rooms were empty?"

"Yeah," said Jane. "She said the doctor likes to live on the upper stories so she can keep an eye on the town."

"So if Alinor's here," I said slowly, "she may be up at the top."

"And if we can trust Mrs. Bock's memory, the staircase should be just beyond that door," said Max.

"Let's review the procedure," I said.

"OK," said Max. "Our goal is to simply discover whether or not she's here."

"Right. We'll check the lower rooms pretty carefully."

"And quietly," added Max.

We tiptoed across the large room by the light of the flickering candle. Max was in the lead. Just as his fingers grasped the handle of the great door I saw something I hadn't noticed before—a thread-thin shaft of light under the door.

"Max!" I hissed.

Too late. Max saw the light too, but only after he had pulled the door open. It swung creakingly inward. The room beyond was brightly lit with a chandelier of candles.

I noticed the candles first because they were the brightest objects. But once I'd blinked a couple times, my eyes focused on something else.

A dark figure stood in the doorway. I shaded my eyes and hiccuped. Max leaped backward, nearly knocking me over.

There before us, a cocked and loaded crossbow at the ready, a quiver full of bolts slung behind his shoulder, stood the baron.

23

The baron stared at us, the snout of his crossbow aimed directly at my stomach.

"How you got in here, Anwyck, I do not know," he finally said in the harsh voice I remembered so well. "But now that you're in, you can join the princess."

"So Alinor's here?" Jane asked.

The baron chuckled mirthlessly. "Of course, she's here. What she thought she was going to accomplish at the Wyndhameshire palace, I couldn't say. Let's just say she was intercepted as she left the farm." He stepped backward into the brightly lit room. His eyes never wavering from mine. "Follow me. Move very carefully."

One by one Max, Jane, and then I filed into the room after him. When the baron finally diverted his gaze, I flicked a glance into a hallway to the right. I could see moonlight through a huge door that stood partly ajar.

"Don't get any ideas, Anwyck," grated the baron.

My eyes met his again.

He chuckled mirthlessly. "If you know what's good for you, you won't try to make a break for it."

"Where's Alinor?" Jane asked.

The baron looked Jane up and down. "You'll be joining her shortly. And," he added, "don't imagine that your friend Sir Robert is suddenly going to ride to the rescue. I've just come from the Wyndhamshire palace, where I've been watching nonstop for more than 24 hours. He went in yesterday, and I haven't seen him since. I assume he's occupying one of the excellent dungeons beneath the palace."

He walked over to stand between us and the outside door. "Up you go," he snarled, gesturing with his crossbow toward a gigantic spiral staircase that wound upward into the darkness.

We paused.

He raised the crossbow higher and aimed it at my heart. "Anwyck, I know you're a cunning little weasel. You proved that a month ago at my castle, and just the other day at that grocer's shop. But this time—" he paused significantly—"there's no chance I'll miss. *Up those stairs!*"

My knees had turned to water. I reached for the handrail and pulled myself upward, step by step. *Must it end like this?* I asked myself in despair. Over the centuries many dark deeds had been done and wars begun in towers like this. And now our two countries would descend into war, and no one would ever know the truth of what happened tonight.

At the end of the first spiral, the baron spoke again. "Don't stop climbing. If you're thinking of jumping out one of those windows, you'll kill yourself even if I miss you. There's no reason to escape. When I shouted to the doctor, that was the signal to give the princess a dose of poison. You will probably not find her alive when you get to the top."

My fists tightened, and as they did so I felt the cloth Jane had wrapped around my injured knuckles. Suddenly, illogically, my knees became strong. I wanted to leap upward, three steps at a time, vaulting to the top. If I could just get to Alinor!

"Slow down, Anwyck!" barked the baron. "If you run,

I throw your friends down the stairwell to their death."

I forced myself to slacken my pace. Finally, high in the dark tower, we arrived at a closed door.

"Open it," rasped the baron.

Max pushed it open. Again our eyes were struck by the blaze of a chandelier, even brighter than the one below. I stepped inside.

The room was large and circular, with a bed at one side and several upright cabinets and chests. Seated in a chair, her back to us, staring out upon the moonlit town, was the lanky, familiar figure of an old woman with wild white locks and hooked nose. Like a fierce bird of prey she looked quickly around at us. For a second her eyes gleamed, not with surprise and anger as I'd thought they might, but with puzzlement and confusion.

I glanced around the room, and my eyes focused more clearly on the bed. "Alinor!" I cried out.

My friend lay bound hand and foot, her back to me, her dark gold hair splayed out on a white pillow. She stirred slightly, then became still again. I froze where I stood, as if in a dream.

"She's sleeping," croaked the doctor.

The baron pushed Max and Jane into the room and slammed the door behind him. Dr. Skotia stared at him. Again I noticed that look of puzzlement.

Jane glanced at Alinor and darted across the room. "What did you give her?" she screamed.

The baron leaped after her, slapping her away with such force that she tumbled and rolled across the floor, coming to rest close to my feet.

"Stand up," snapped the baron.

Max and I quickly lifted Jane to her feet. Her face was white except for a dusky red mark across one cheekbone.

The baron raised his crossbow. "Turn your backs to me," he ordered in a voice of deadly calm. "Doctor, you may wish to look elsewhere for a moment. This will not take long."

Together we turned our faces to the wall.

Suddenly there was a knock at the door, a mild, almost humble knock. But there was something insistent about it. The doctor uttered a wordless cry.

"Who is that?" the baron whispered.

I turned. As the crossbow trembled in his grasp, for a second I debated leaping upon him. But he quickly regained his composure and, raising his crossbow again, he strode across the room and flung the door open.

There stood my king. He was still clad in the wonderfully familiar robe he was wearing when he stood in the moonlight the night before, but this time he wore no hood. I knew for certain that one strip of cloth from that hood was bandaged tightly around Jane's hand another around mine.

It was that cloth that had given me such courage when I needed it in the room below. It had strengthened my faith that no matter how bad things were, my king was close by, and I need not worry.

The king seemed unworried too, even though the deadly point of a crossbow arrow now hovered barely six feet from his chest. He stood mildly, as though he were an invited guest. The only thing unguestlike about his attire was the four-foot scabbard buckled to his left thigh, from the top of which protruded a giant silver sword handle.

"Mordred," he said calmly. "Remember who I am. Remember what I taught you. Remember that I see treasure in the heart of even my bitterest enemy."

The baron wordlessly raised the crossbow to his shoulder and aimed it directly at the king's heart, sighting along its top as carefully as if his target were 100 yards away.

"Mordred," the king said softly, "there is still time."

"I have no more time for you," the baron spat out in a

taut, small voice. "I killed your son. Your granddaughter lies on that bed, dying from poison. And I would kill them both again and again if I could."

"Why?"

The baron shook his head impatiently. "Prepare yourself to die!"

"Speak with me, Mordred. Reason with me."

"No! I now claim your kingdom. You must follow your son."

His hand tightened suddenly on the iron trigger beneath the crossbow. A deadly *twang* echoed through the room.

Jane screamed. The crossbow bolt jutted horizontally from the king's chest, trembling and heaving horribly. His Majesty staggered back, then regained his balance. He stood silent for a moment, then reached up and twitched the arrow away.

"Have you forgotten," he said, smiling sadly, "that Martin the smith double-weaves my chain mail?"

Suddenly, with apparently no motion, the king's tremendous silver sword flashed in his right hand. As he raised it, his robe fell away to expose the gleaming iron rings of chain mail beneath it.

"Doctor," said His Majesty urgently, "what has Alinor been given?"

"Only a dose of sleeping powder, Your Majesty, to keep her quiet," croaked the old woman. "She will awaken in a few minutes."

The baron whirled, flung down his crossbow, and towered over Dr. Skotia.

"Mordred, no closer." The king's sword flashed in the candlelight.

The baron ignored him. "Why did you disobey me?" he snarled down at the doctor.

"Thirteen years ago I delivered that child," she said

simply. "I do not take back a life that I have brought into the world."

The baron stared at her for five heartbeats, then dove for his crossbow. The king's sword flashed out again, severing the bowstring. The baron lunged for the loose arrow, raising it in his fists and thrusting it at the king. Another slash from His Majesty's blade clipped its point off cleanly.

"It is no use, Mordred," said the king calmly. "The palace guard waits for you on the lawn outside."

24

"Denis." Max shoved a golden platter toward me across the mahogany table. "Want some more scrambled eggs?"

"Eat up, there," cackled a tiny old gentleman at the table's head. "You're a growing boy. That's what I used to tell Andrew."

It was 10:00 in the morning, the day after the midnight tower adventure, and I was seated at a huge table in the great hall of the Wyndhamshire king's palace.

Early this morning, after a hasty ride from the tower on the palace guards' horses, we'd been ushered through the huge front door of the palace, where King Randall had hurried us to bed. "No questions until you get some sleep," he had insisted.

And now, as I finished my final helping of scrambled eggs, I glanced around the huge table. At its head sat the little Wyndhamshire monarch, a balding gnome with a huge nose. My own king was seated beside him, wearing an expression of peace and deep satisfaction on his lined face. Next to him sat Alinor, pale but surprisingly restored after last night's adventures. I was next to her, and on my other side sat Max, with Jane beside him. Across from us were Sir Robert, Mrs. Bock, and Squire Forster.

King Randall peered over his giant nose at us. "All right," he began, "I promised you a question-and-answer

time after breakfast. Of course, since my fellow monarch explained things to me so persuasively yesterday, I now know the truth about Andrew and Geoffrey. And I know a little of the rest of the story, such as how the baron found some sort of royal seal and set someone to watch his town house where the princess was staying."

"It was careless of me to lose it," said Alinor.

Her grandfather nodded. "It was."

"The mysterious vendor was a certain Sir Cedric," continued King Randall. "He is—or was—one of the baron's knights. But after he was ordered to poison Alinor, he began to have second thoughts about the baron's plans."

Max frowned. "Then Sir Cedric must have been the one who cut the underbraces. But when could he have done that? And how could he have known we were going to Wyndhamshire?"

King Randall chuckled. "You kept your secret well. It was pure luck that he found out. Cedric watched the town house until nearly midnight that night. When nothing seemed to be happening, he decided to return to a friend's house where he was boarding."

"So he never suspected we'd escaped out the back door?" asked Alinor, her eyes dancing.

"No, princess. But as he was riding his horse toward his friend's house, he saw His Majesty walking along the road from the castle."

Alinor's grandfather nodded thoughtfully. "I *thought* someone was following me."

"And therefore, Your Majesty," said Sir Robert, "he saw you stop the longwagon and speak briefly with me."

"Right," King Randall said. "He heard someone mention Wyndhamshire and the palace, and he immediately went and told the baron. The two of them hurried back, and since there's only one road a carriage would take to

Wyndhamshire, they rode along until they caught up with you. After you were asleep, Sir Cedric crept up and sabotaged the carriage."

"But why damage the underbraces at all?" puzzled Sir Robert. "What were they trying to achieve?"

"The baron wanted to kidnap the princess, or perhaps even do away with her, but he didn't want witnesses. So he figured if the underbrace broke, you and one of the boys might ride ahead to the village for help. And that would make it easier for him to attack."

"He didn't know that Charles Judde had not only sent along a spare underbrace, but also a fine son who had been trained in the highest quality of workmanship, and who took his responsibilities very seriously," Alinor's grandfather said.

"It was then," resumed King Randall, "that Sir Cedric refused to have anything further to do with the scheme. He escaped and laid low in his friend's house for a while until he could get enough funds together to come over here. He just arrived this morning and has been very helpful in filling in the details."

Squire Forster took up the story. "At this point the baron decided to ignore the carriage and travel directly to Wyndhamshire himself. He took a shortcut—a steep mountain pass that only the best horsemen use—and arrived in Wyndhamshire well before the carriage did. He didn't know where the carriage would be parked, but he assumed that Sir Robert would go directly to the palace. So he disguised himself and watched the front gate of the royal grounds."

Sir Robert turned toward the king. "Your Majesty is to be commended for his foresight in asking Mrs. Bock for her hospitality."

"Our thanks to you, Mrs. Bock," said my king. "And

again, my deepest condolences at the death of your husband."

She smiled tremulously at him.

"When evil and good collide," His Majesty continued softly, "the losses are sometimes very real and very permanent." He put his arm around Alinor and hugged her to him.

Sir Robert cleared his throat. "Eventually, Denis and I did show up at the palace. And since we were sent out by the servants' entrance at the rear, the baron didn't know we'd gone. So he must have still been waiting there when Alinor rode by on her way to the cemetery."

Alinor's grandfather nodded, his eyes on me.

"Yes," I said in a low voice, "and if I had followed His Majesty's directions she wouldn't have got shot."

Alinor turned to me, tears in her eyes. "I forgive you," she said. "I'm more to blame than anyone else for not listening to Grandpa." She turned and looked into her grandfather's eyes. "You told us that you had many things under your control. I should have believed you."

He pulled her toward him in another hug. "Now you understand how right I was."

"But how," asked King Randall, "did Dr. Skotia get mixed up in this?"

Alinor's grandfather smiled sadly. "Dr. Skotia is not always in her right mind. In her medical experiments she has used much mercury, and its fumes are not good for the brain. In one of her weak moments the baron convinced her to help him."

"What will happen to her?" Alinor asked softly.

"There is a physician in Costello who cares for the mildly insane," said her grandfather. "She is being taken there now. Perhaps with rest and relief from stress, she may improve."

King Randall stared at the table expressionlessly. "For this our two sons died."

The room was silent for a long moment.

My king took up the tale. "The baron didn't realize that I came to this country two days ago," he said. "Squire Forster's visit to my castle gave me all the evidence I needed to convince my friend Randall of the baron's plot, so I traveled back with Forster. We arrived at the Bock farm late at night and decided not to wake anyone."

"And you talked together beside the barn," I said excitedly. "At first I thought it was a dream, but you dropped the hood of your robe there, and Jane found it next day. When I saw it, I suddenly knew everything would turn out all right, because you were near."

He smiled at Jane. "Jane, you have done much good on this trip. I thank you for employing your skills when Alinor was in danger."

"Yes," said King Randall, "and if your king doesn't get his bid in first, I'd like your services as my physician in a few years."

Jane smiled in a rather dazed way. "Thank you," she said, in the softest voice I'd ever heard her use.

"Immediately after I left the Bock farm," our king continued, "I went to the palace dressed as a peddler and gained entrance at the back gate. Sir Robert was already in the palace—he'd done such good diplomatic work that Randall had allowed him to stay the night. Once inside, I showed my royal seal, and Randall and I began to have some earnest conversations.

"All this time, of course, the baron was watching the palace—not knowing that he himself was being closely watched by the palace guard. When he finally returned to the tower last night, a small patrol followed him here, and others alerted me. I followed as quickly as I could. Since at that time no one knew you young people had entered the tower, the guard simply waited on the lawn."

"But who set my cottage on fire? And why?" Mrs. Bock asked.

"Again, it was the baron," said Sir Robert. "He was visiting the doctor and was with her atop her tower on the day the young people went to the grocer's. Dr. Skotia noticed Jane and mentioned to the baron that she had seen Jane at Mrs. Bock's house. So as soon as he fired at Alinor on the grocer's doorstep and missed, he turned and shot a fire arrow into Mrs. Bock's roof. It wasn't a difficult shot as the cottage is only two or three blocks from the doctor's tower. He hoped to destroy Alinor's place of refuge."

"Seems to me," King Randall commented, "that these young people deserve credit for all they've done."

"They do," agreed my king, and smiled at us. "And Alinor, your quest to find the truth about your father has been successful."

"Grandpa," said Alinor, "I have a question."

"What is it, my child?"

She clenched her hands tightly in her lap, and her chin trembled slightly. In a voice barely audible to the rest of us, she asked, "What if I fail you again?"

The king's great hand engulfed both of hers, and his gentle eyes moved around the room to include us all. "Each of you put yourself in my service. And though some of you made very dangerous mistakes by ignoring what I'd told you, you braved your fears and used your talents to serve me well."

"But Grandpa," her voice held an almost desperate intensity, "do you still love me?"

"Yes, my child. There has never been a time when I did not."

The king rose to his feet. "And now, my little princess, let us begin our journey home."